KEITH WATERHOUSE

Keith Waterhouse is one of our most distinguished and popular writers. He has provided a wide range of work for television, cinema and the theatre, and writes an award-winning column for the *Daily Mail*. His play JEFFREY BERNARD IS UNWELL has been one of the most successful productions of recent years on the London stage and his novels, which include BILLY LIAR, BIMBO and most recently UNSWEET CHARITY, have been published to great acclaim.

Keith Waterhouse is also the author of several works of non-fiction including THE THEORY AND PRACTICE OF TRAVEL and a collection of his journalism, SHARON & TRACY & THE REST, published by Hodder and Stoughton.

sceptre

Keith Waterhouse

THERE IS A HAPPY LAND

First published in Great Britain in 1957 by Michael Joseph Ltd

Sceptre edition 1992

Sceptre is an imprint of Hodder and Stoughton Paperbacks, a division of Hodder and Stoughton Ltd

Printed and bound in Great Britain for Hodder and Stoughton Paperbacks, a division of Hodder and Stoughton Ltd, Mill Road, Dunton Green, Sevenoaks, Kent TN13 2YA. (Editorial Office: 47 Bedford Square, London WC1B 3DP) by Clays Ltd, St Ives plc.

A CIP catalogue record for this book is available from the British Library

ISBN 0-340-57463-1

1

IT was better than Christmas, the way we rolled off down the road, shouting and bawling and pretending to limp as though we had cork legs like Mr Bailey. Ted rattled his stick against the railings and chanted: 'Little bit of spice cake, little bit of cheese; glass of cold water, a *penny* if you please. If you haven't got a penny, halfpenny will do; if you haven't got a halfpenny your door's going through.'

A woman shouted from out of their garden: 'Make a less noise, pair of you! You're like I don't know what!'

She was sitting in an armchair near their gate with all her big fat legs showing. There was a big furniture van outside and all carpets in the road and that. They must have been removing. 'Hey, missus, your shirt lap's hanging out!' shouted Ted. We were miles away from where we lived, so nobody could say anything. We started yodelling at her and making burping noises; then we went on down the road, walking bow-legged and singing Christmas carols.

> *While shepherds watched their turnip tops*
> *A-boiling in the pot,*
> *An angel of the Lord came down*
> *And scoffed the blinking lot.*

'Have we to go carol-singing outside Old Ma Theaker's, see if she gives us anything?' said Ted.

'Chuck a bucket of water over us, that's all she *would* give us,' I said.

> *Good King Wenceslas*
> *Knocked a bobby senseless*
> *Right in the middle of Marks and Spencers . . .*

It was in the middle of July and right hot. No, June it must have been, because not that Saturday, but the Saturday after, Ted's mother was taking us to the pantomime. The pantos went on all through summer up where we lived, but they didn't run into July, I know that much, because that's when the Royal Players started. Anyway, whatever month it was we'd been getting newts out of that pond near where the quarries are. We were walking up Parkside, just before you get to our school.

'Have we to talk in Arjy Parjy?' said Ted.

Arjy Parjy was like a secret language we had in our class. You had to put 'arj' in the middle of every word, and if you could speak it fast you were right good.

'Darjo yarjou sparjeak Arjy Parjy?' I said.

'Yarjes. Darjo yarjou?'

We walked back up the road as far as the furniture van and shouted to the woman in the armchair: 'Darjo yarjou sparjeak Arjy Parjy?' She shouted: 'Wait till I go down to that school! You'll be laughing on the other side of your faces!' We shouted: 'Couldn't catch a copper!' and crossed over the road, seeing how straight we could go walking backwards.

'Carjan yarjou sparjeak Arjy Parjy as warjell as marjee?' said Ted.

'Yarjes, I carjan sparjeak it barjetter tharjan any-barjony,' I said.

6

'*I-i-it* isn't anybarjony. I mean, it arjisn't anybarjony,' said Ted. 'It's anybarjody.'

'*Said* anybarjody.'

'Yarjou darjidn't.'

'Darjid.'

'Darjidn't.'

'Darjid.'

We walked on past the branch library, just before you get to our street. Ted puts his hands to his mouth and bawls out: 'Got any books to give away?' and it echoed back at us.

'Smashed windows, by Eva Brick,' I said.

'What a smell, by Hoo Flung Dung,' said Ted.

'A walk in the woods, by Theresa Green.'

'No, this is it. A walk in the woods by Theresa Brown.'

'No. A walk in the woods by Theresa Tall.'

'Walk in the woods by Theresa Smelly.'

'Warjalk in the warjoods by Theresa Smarjelly.'

We got down as far as our street, Coronation Grove. Ted was frightened to go in because he'd got all mud over his stockings, so we squatted down on the edge of the road and started flattening tar bubbles. We had some of these like sticks they use for tying up plants with and we started seeing how far out into the road we could get with them without moving.

Soon popped all the bubbles we could reach, so we had to start leaning right out to get at the big bubbles in the middle of the road. You couldn't get *up*, but you could lean out as far as you wanted without leaving the edge of the road.

'No putting hands on the road!' shouted Ted. It was

dead easy if you put one hand on the road to steady yourself with.

I said: 'Who's *put*ting their hands on the road?' He was only jealous because I had popped more bubbles than him, so he starts putting *his* hand on the road and getting at bubbles miles out in the middle of the street.

I shouted: 'Yur, look who's talking!' and started knocking his stick away with mine. We both fell forward into the road, hitting at each other's sticks. 'Fencing!' shouts Ted. He puts one hand behind his back and starts jabbing at my stomach with his stick. 'Two Japanese wrestlers!' I said, and came back at him. We worked our way right out into the middle of the road. Ted started trying to knock my stick out of my hand and shouted: 'Robin Hood and his merry men!' I was just going to get his stick off him when all of a sudden I saw this blinking bike pelting down the street, swerving so that it wouldn't run into us.

I shouted: 'Mind that feller's bike!' but it was too late. Ted swished his stick back ready to knock mine out of my hand. It went straight through the blinking spokes on this fellow's front wheel. The bike went up in the air and this fellow just managed to get his foot out on to the ground to stop himself from falling. Good job he wasn't going all that fast, else he'd have gone clean over the handlebars.

We just stood there, waiting for him to play pop with us. He didn't say anything, though. Didn't even tell us off for playing round the fever drains. He just looked at us, winked, and made this noise out of the side of his mouth.

'Grr-*quack*!'

I can't do it, because it's not a noise that anything

makes, not even a duck. It was a sort of cross between a quack and a tiger, but it was a nice noise, I suppose. He just sat on the cross-bar, pulled his bike up straight and made this noise. He didn't smile: he just winked and went: 'Qua-ack! Grr-qua-ack!'

He was a big fellow with a shiny red face and sort of gingery hair, but not so much that you could shout 'Gin'er' after him. It was like a dirty colour. I don't think he had many teeth, and they were all yellow, what I could see of them when he made this noise. He wore an old blazer that looked as though he'd had it given, and flannels that weren't even tucked into his socks to stop getting oil on them off the bicycle chain. He had hair coming out of his ears.

'Grr-*quack*!' he went for the *third* time. Then he rides off down the street on this bike, leaving Ted's stick in bits in the middle of the road. He was riding all over the shop, first on one side of the road and then on the other. Bet his front wheel was buckled.

'Hey, mister, your back wheel's following your front!' shouted Ted, but he couldn't hear us. Just before he got to the corner of Royal Park Crescent he sticks his leg out at right angles to show he was turning. There were a couple more kids near our lamp-post and he made this noise at them as well.

Me and Ted stood and stared till he was out of sight then we both started laughing and shouting and mocking this fellow. 'Grr-*quack*!' 'No, this is it. Grr-r *quack*!' 'No. Grr-*qua*-ack!'

We set off home, sticking our legs out like we had seen this man do and making this noise. Ted never used to know when to stop and he started going 'Grr-*quack*!' at all the blinking rotten neighbours. *He* was all right, because he lived further down the street from us and they didn't know him. Anyway, Mrs Theaker saw us and said we were cheeky, and she knew his mother so he stopped after that.

We walked properly as far as the next telegraph pole, not even daring to look at each other, then we both burst out laughing at the same time, the laughter spurting out of us like a balloon being let down.

'Grr-*quack*!'

'No, look, man! Grr-*quack*!'

'No. Grr-*qua*-ack!'

Ted grabbed my stick and put it between his legs and pretended it was this man's bicycle. He put one leg out, trying to look as if he was turning round a corner, and then he found he had got all tar all over his trousers. He starts holding the seat of his trousers out with his hands and going: '*Yerks*! Look what you've blinking done, man!' I started doing it as well, and it was like this—both going: 'Yerks! *Yerks*, man!' as loud as we could, and staggering about holding our trousers seats out—that we got as far as Ted's house.

Just as we were going in their gate he said: 'If my mother wants to know how I got all this tar on, it was your stick that did it, not mine.' Just like him, blames it all on to me. Pinches my stick off me and then says it was my fault. He was my best friend, was Ted, but I hated him sometimes. He was all right, but he was awkward in a lot of ways. He lived right down at the bottom of our street, down in the two hundreds, just past that black doctor's. Well, it was always me that had to call for him, never him that called for me. And he could hit you, but you couldn't hit him. And if he ever got into cop it, it was always your fault.

Another thing about Ted, he was always saying things about people, but you just say anything about him and he used to turn on you. He used to come up to you and go: 'Do you want this button?' and if you used to say yes, well he used to pull the blinking thing off your coat and give it to you, but if you said no, well he used to pull it off and throw it away. Then he'd go: 'Well, you said you didn't want it!' You try doing anything like that with him, though. You never knew how far you could go with Ted.

Anyway, we get to their back door and it's blinking locked. His mother must have been out shopping. Ted wanted me to stay with him till she came back, in case she said anything about him dirtying his best clothes. I didn't mind staying, because it wasn't *my* blinking fault he'd got tar on his trousers. Tell you what I *did* mind though, and that was Ted sitting on their step and reciting one of these stupid sayings that go round. He used to get them out of the *Rover* and the *Wizard* and that. He was always going:

'How much wood could a wood-chuck chuck if a wood-chuck could chuck wood?' and things like that. It was all right anybody else doing them, but whenever Ted used to do it, it always used to make me feel awkward, don't know why.

I laughed, a sniggering sort of laugh, and said: 'You *what*?'

'If-your-Bob-doesn't-give-our-Bob-that-Bob-that-your-Bob-owes-our-Bob-our-Bob's-going-to-give-your-Bob-a-bob-over-the-ear.' He said it very quickly. He was always saying these stupid sayings very quickly.

I said: 'If your Bob *what*?' feeling silly.

'Aw, you want to wash your ears out, man!' said Ted.

He started showing off and recited it quicker and quicker till he tripped up over some of the words. I laughed at him, so of course he didn't like it then.

'Hey, vaulting over your wall!' I said, to try and take Ted's mind off these stupid sayings. He used to keep a vaulting-pole propped up near their dustbin. We used to vault over their garden wall with it.

Another thing about Ted, he always wanted everything to himself. He got out the vaulting-pole and started vaulting over their wall with it. I kept shouting: '*Give* us a go, man!' but he wouldn't take any notice. He wouldn't give me a go.

I had to stand there like a fool, watching him vault backwards and forwards into Mathieson's garden and shouting: 'You wait till old Ma Mathieson comes out at him!' After a bit he says: 'Vaulting over our front gate!' so I have to traipse out to the front gate with him and watch him vaulting over *that*.

After he'd had it for ages, Ted let me have the pole. 'Only one go!' he said. I went out into the street with it and took a flying leap over the gate into their garden. One of my feet just caught the head of a Michaelmas daisy.

'Aw, you've done it now, man!' cried Ted. 'Caw, look what you've done with your big feet!'

'*I-it's* nothing!' I said, getting nervous. I had only broken the head of one flower.

'Oh, isn't it! Trust you! Wait till my mother finds out, that's all. Well it was you! I'm not going to say it was me.'

'Not asking you to.'

'Not *off* to, so you needn't think I am!'

'Don't *want* you to.'

He got down and started messing about with this flower. It wasn't *worth* twopence when it was *there*.

Then all of a sudden he gets up and starts acting daft again. 'Anyway, we've done it now,' he said. He aimed his boot at the broken flower and kicked the head clean off it. He got his vaulting-pole and started swishing it at the other flowers, just missing the tops of them. Then he starts doing it at *me*, swinging the pole about two inches over my head.

I called out: '*Mind* out, man!' Ted pretended to be out of the lunatic asylum and started pulling his funny face. 'You'll *go* like it!' I said. He started squinting his eyes and lolling his tongue out and taking swipes at me with this vaulting-pole. It was a heavy pole that used to be a scout staff. He just missed me every time.

After a bit he dropped the pole and started mincing round the garden like a girl. He pulled his trousers up high up to his thighs like tights and pranced round holding the legs up with his hands.

'If *youah* Robert does not give *ouah* Robert that shilling that *youah* Robert owes *ouah* Robert,' he went, in a high-pitched, la-di-da sort of voice. I said: 'You'll *go* like it, man!' Then I started copying him and said: 'Oh, *reahlly*!' in the same voice. Ted suddenly stopped and became King Kong, dropping his arms in front of him and snarling like an ape. Then he was a monkey, scratching himself under the arms and making cackling noises.

'Hey, two monkeys having a fight!' he said suddenly. I had to pretend to be a monkey and we started rolling on the ground pretending to wrestle.

That started it, supposed to be only playing, but

you try just playing with *him*. He was all right for a minute then he starts biting. He kept getting his teeth into my arm and worrying it. Well, it didn't hurt, but after a bit I noticed bits of spit on my sleeve. I went: 'You-ou—look what you've done!' and wiped it off on his jersey. Ted went: '*Mu-ucky* devil!' I said: 'See how *you* like it!' and bending down to the ground I bit his bare leg. I bit a lot deeper than I thought and he shouted: 'Ge-et o-o-off, man! I'm *tell*ing you!'

I let go and I could see the marks of my teeth on his leg. I pretended to be a mad monkey and went: 'Grrrrr-*an*! Grrr-*an*!'

'You're blooming barmy, man!' said Ted.

'Grrrrr-*an*! Grrr-*an*!'

'*Gi-ive* up, crackers!'

'Grrrrr-*an*!'

I suddenly realized that Ted had got his mad up. I felt very silly and stood up, laughing like you do at the very end of a joke.

'Yer, you think you're good, don't you?' snapped Ted.

'Cur, just cos you got bit, man!'

'Yer, well I didn't bite *you* like that!'

'Not much!'

'You just wait if I get blinking blood poisoning,' said Ted.

'Yar-rn—get away, man!' I said.

'Yer, it's all right for you!'

He kept going on about it, just because he'd got hurt for once. Anyway, he finished up saying: 'And you needn't think my mother's taking you to that pantomime, so you know!' I was supposed to be going to the Theatre Royal with Ted and his mother a week that Saturday, and after that to Church Moor Feast. She used to take us every year.

'Don't want her to, I can go on my own!' I said. I was feeling hurt, but on the top of it, angry.

'She's not *going* to, don't *you* worry!' said Ted. Then he said: 'You're nothing but a bloody bugger when you're there!'

'Same to you with knobs on,' I said. I felt myself going red.

'*Shu-ut* up, bloody bugger!'

'Shut up yourself!'

'Don't you tell *me* to shut up, bloody bugger! And you can get out of our garden as well!'

I said: 'I'm *going*, don't *you* worry.' I walked to the gate. Ted followed after me, limping where I had bitten him in the leg.

He shouted after me: 'And you needn't think you're getting your whirrer back, either!' He'd got my whirrer. It was like a piece of string with a lead weight at the end. It made a whirring noise when you swung it round.

I called back: 'I don't *want* it back, so you can keep it!' I wondered how I was going to get my whirrer back.

'You're not *get*ting it!'

I shouted: 'And you're not getting your joke book back, either, so you needn't think you are!'

'Oh, but I am!'

'You're not, you know!'

'Pity you if I don't!' shouted Ted. 'You wait!'

I walked off up the street, not looking round. A stone came whizzing past and just missed me.

I thought about my quarrel with Ted all the way up Coronation Grove, thinking of me calling *him* a bloody bugger and imagining me getting drowned saving Theaker's dog in Park Lake and him being sorry. No, this is it—saving *him* from being drowned and walking away without speaking after I had got him out.

Up near our lamp-post I saw this furniture van that had been up in Parkside that afternoon, where we were mocking that woman. It was standing outside where Braithwaites used to live, next door to us. I imagined me getting run over with it and having my legs off, and Ted mocking me and spitting at me, and me just watching him with tears in my eyes because I couldn't move.

Braithwaites' had been empty for ages. They had a telegraph pole in their garden. They were dirty. They had to have the bug-van when they removed. Anyway, the house didn't look empty now, because two men were lifting a sideboard up the path out of this van, and I could see rolls of lino leaning up against the front-room window. I suddenly remembered how we'd been shouting arjy parjy at this woman earlier on, and I thought: 'Pity me if she's coming to live next door to us!'

I watched the removal van for a bit, then I looked round our street to see if there was anyone I could get a game of hiddy with. There was nobody in sight, so I thought I'd go in.

I went in through our garden and round to the back door, and the first thing I clap eyes on is this blinking fat woman that we'd been shouting names at, talking to my Auntie Betty. I was scared stiff. I was just going to dodge back round the corner of the house when my Auntie Betty sees me and shouts: 'Come back here! I want you!'

'Wasn't going anywhere,' I mumbled. I drew in my lower lip and tried to look as though I had horse teeth so this woman couldn't tell it was me.

My Auntie Betty didn't take any more notice of me, just went on talking to this woman.

'Here, who's that man who's always on that bicycle —does *he* live in Parkside?' my Auntie Betty said.

'Who do you mean, him that sticks his leg out?' the woman said. She was staring straight at me. I remembered how Ted had shouted: 'Hey, missus, your shirt lap's hanging out' at her, and hoped she didn't think it was me who'd shouted it.

Thought I could get in with them by joining in what they were talking about, so I chimed in: 'Is it him that makes that funny noise?'

'I don't know what kind of a noise he makes,' my Auntie Betty said. 'I wonder if he lives in them houses in Carnegie Road.'

I said: 'I don't know, but I know he was going round by Royal Park Crescent when *we* saw him.' Felt like saying: 'We've been down Royal Park Crescent all after*noon*,' so this woman would think it was someone else who'd been shouting after her, but I thought I'd better not after all.

'He'll live in them new houses,' my Auntie Betty said.

'I think he's a bit simple, if it's him that I'm thinking of,' the woman said. She was standing there with her arms folded. She looked as though she was going to be there for the rest of the night.

'He's not simple, he's blinking crackers,' I said.

Don't know why I came out with that, because I might have known what was coming.

'Don't you be so cheeky!' my Auntie Betty said. 'You've too much off! And what were you shouting at this lady this afternoon?'

I suddenly felt like running to the lavatory. Didn't know the woman had already *told* my Auntie Betty about us.

'Shouting what?' I said.

'You know very well what!' my Auntie Betty went. 'What were you shouting?'

'Wasn't shouting *any*thing. It was Ted. I was just with him, that's all.'

'No, it was both of them,' this woman says, sticking *her* oar in. 'Because I took particular notice. I was going to go down to the school about them.'

'They're both as bad as each other,' my Auntie Betty said. 'I'm going to get him sent away if he doesn't stop calling after people. What were you *shout*ing?' she said to me again. The woman said: 'I'll get back to my furniture.'

I started crying. I went: 'I wasn't shouting at all, and I'm off to run away!' then I ducked past them and pelted up to the top of our garden. There was a big hole there that I'd been digging for weeks, trying to see how far down you could get, and I jumped in it and sat there, just waiting for my Auntie Betty to call me in again. It was about six feet deep and you couldn't get out again without using these footholds. I sat on this plank at the bottom and imagined me stopping there all night and my Auntie Betty finding my dead body in the morning and remembering that her last words to me had been: 'I'll give you something to cry about when I get hold of you!'

2

So that was *that* day. Got told off for shouting out at this woman, and my Auntie Betty told me I hadn't to go out of our street till she let me.

Next day I thought I might as well go down past Ted's so that if he was in their garden, well, I could walk straight past him without speaking. Wanted to have a squint at him anyway, just in case he'd got blood poisoning in his leg where I'd bitten him. I started rehearsing what I'd say to my Auntie Betty if he had to go into the Infirmary. I could say I slipped and my teeth just caught in his leg. I remembered where he'd started it by biting me first, right on my arm, and I wondered whether it would be worth my while to cut my elbow with some mucky old glass so that I'd get worse blood poisoning than him, then nobody could say anything. I wrestled my arm out of my coat sleeve and tucked the sleeve into my pocket so that Ted would think I'd had to have my arm off, then I set off down Coronation Grove.

Get down as far as where Braithwaites used to live, where that fat woman had just moved in. Thought I'd better cross over the road just in case she was looking out of their window. There was a pair of steps in the window where they were putting the curtains up, and I thought she might see me and start playing pop again. I was just crossing over the street when I saw this girl coming out of their gate. Never seen her before. She was about as old as me, but she was different from all the other kids in our street. I mean, she was like neat and tidy and that. She had right light-coloured hair that looked as though she'd just had it washed, and she was wearing like a green velvet dress. It was a bit like our tablecloth. It was all right.

It was too late to walk straight past her so I stopped and said: 'We're tracing a man in a fawn raincoat. Has he been past here?'

She thought I was a detective. '*I* haven't seen anybody,' she said.

'Just checking up,' I said. 'Well, report to us if you see him. I'd have caught up with him by now if it wasn't for my arm.' I patted my sleeve where I'd wrestled my arm out of it.

'What's up with it?'

'Broke it,' I said.

'What on?'

'Racing down Clarkson's Hill on a bus tyre,' I said.

'Oo, poor old you.'

'It's nearly better now, though,' I said. Thought I'd better say that, just in case she saw me the next day with my arm out again.

She sat on their gate and started swinging her legs. She was wearing white ankle socks, not mucky old brown stockings like some people.

'You've only just come to live here, haven't you?' I said.

'Yes.'

'You used to live down Parkside, didn't you?'

'Yes. It's you that was calling after my mother when we were removing, isn't it?'

'Wasn't me at all, then, clever clogs, it was that kid who was with me,' I said, sticking my chin out. 'Just cos I was there, I get all the blame for it.'

'I bet it *was* you all the time,' she said.

'Was not. How could it have been me when I've broke my arm?'

'Don't shout with your arm, dafthead,' she said.

'Maybe not, but it makes a difference to your voice,' I said.

She lost interest in my arm and said: 'What do they call you?'

Told her my name. 'Anyway, what do they call *you*?' I said.

'Marion Longbottom.'

Felt like saying: 'Why, is your bottom long?' but I thought I'd better not, so I just said 'Aw' instead.

Couldn't think of anything else to say, so I thought I might as well start playing up my broken arm. I pretended it was hurting me and started gripping hold of the railings and biting my lip to stop from crying out, but she didn't take any notice, so I thought I might as well stop.

'Do you ever have any books to swop?' I said.

'Sometimes do, sometimes don't. Why, what have you got?'

'This week's *Dandy* and some *Beanos* and a *Radio Fun* and that.'

'Swop you this week's *Rainbow* for this week's *Dandy*?'

'I-i-if you want,' I said. I didn't read the *Rainbow* any more, too blinking cissy, but I didn't tell *her* that.

'Has it got Keyhole Kate in it?' she said.

'Course it has. It's in every week.'

'I know. Did you see that where she gets her big long nose caught in that keyhole?'

'Yer. It's where she's seeing what this feller's doing and she gets her nose fast, isn't it?'

'Yes. They have to take the door down to get her nose out of the keyhole, don't they?'

'Yer. Hey, where she gets all black round her eye!'

'Where Hungry Horace gets that cake, only it's soap all the time!'

'Where Desperate Dan boils all them cows in the gasworks!'

We talked about comics for a bit then we couldn't remember any more, so we just stood there. She started asking me who lived in all the different houses and I started telling her. She was all right, was Marion.

'Who lives there?'

'A feller.'

'Who lives *there*, then?'

'Mrs Theaker. We take short cuts through their garden where we go over to the basins.'

I started telling her all about the basins. The basins were some like *holes* up in Clarkson's woods. They were like pits with water at the bottom, only this summer they had baked green at the bottom, all cracked. Everybody used to go up on their bikes and ride round inside them. There were about six basins altogether and you had to ride round each one of them, then climb the slope *out* of this basin into the next one. If you missed one out you were yellow. We used to call it the Wall of Death.

'Do you want to go round to Clarkson's woods, have

a look at the Wall of Death?' I said. Thought Ted and some of the others might be there by now. Thought I could borrow somebody's bike and start showing off with it.

'Not bothered,' said Marion.

'Well, *I'm* off,' I said. 'Are you coming or not?'

'Might as well,' she said.

I pulled my poorly arm back into my sleeve—'Must be nearly better by now,' I said—and we set off. I took her the usual way, through Theaker's garden, with old Ma Theaker going: 'And don't come through here again'; *through* the Clerk of Works' department, *over* the rhubarb fields and into the woods that way. If you had a bike, well, you had to go round by Carnegie Road way.

Just as we climbed the wall into Clarkson's woods we could hear the other kids shouting, and Raymond Garnett going: '*O*mmi! *O*mmi!' because he was getting the rabbit punch as per usual.

I said: 'If we see a kid called Ted, don't tell him about my arm because he's not supposed to know.' I started walking in front of Marion in case anyone thought I was with her. We got on to the path leading up to the basins and we could see them all on the first basin. Saw Ted first of all, riding round on Little Rayner's crossbar. Didn't worry me, he can ride round with Little Rayner till Kingdom Come for all I cared. Then there was Mono—his name was Monoghan only we always used to call him Mono; he was riding round the basins on *his* bike. Raymond Garnett's bike was leaning up against a tree while Big Rayner was giving him the rabbit punch. It was only a blinking fairy cycle when it was there.

Nobody took any notice of me and Marion, so I let her stand with me while I saw whose bike I could borrow. Ted wouldn't lend out *his* bike for a start, even if he'd got it with him. Could have told you that without even asking him. Mono's bike belonged to his uncle and he wasn't supposed to have taken it. Raymond Garnett's was a new one, and I knew Little Rayner wouldn't lend us *his*. I shouted: 'Lend us your bike, Mono!' but Mono said: 'Can't, it's not mine,' and went on riding round the basin, slurring his foot round the slope to keep from falling. I said to Marion: 'Watch me get Garno's!' Might have been only a fairy cycle, but it was a brand new Raleigh. It had a new saddlebag, and shock-absorbers on the handlebars, and one of these like plates over the chain. It was brand new. I shouted: 'Can we borrow your grid, Garno?' Big Rayner, who had got Raymond Garnett in a halfnelson by now, shouted back: 'No, he's given it to me for keeps. Haven't you, Garno? *Have*n't you?' '*O*mmi!' went Garno.

Then Little Rayner rides up with Ted on his crossbar. 'Who's that lass?' he said.

'*I* don't know,' I said. 'They call her Marion Longbottom, I think.'

'Why, is her bottom long?' said Little Rayner. Marion was watching Big Rayner braying Raymond Garnett, and she didn't hear.

Ted jumped down off Little Rayner's crossbar and tried to put on a limp where I'd bit him. He didn't say anything to me, just looked at Little Rayner and said: 'What's *he* want?'

I said: 'What's up with him, can't I come into the woods if I want now?'

Ted still didn't look at me, he just said to Little Rayner: 'Ask him if he's coming to that pantomime with my mother a week on Saturday.'

'Tell him I'm not bothered,' I said to Little Rayner. We always used to talk to each other like that when we fell out.

'Well, tell him if he's going he's to be down at our house for two o'clock, and if he isn't he can stop away,' said Ted. He walked off, forgetting to limp. I heard him shouting to Mono: 'Hey, Mono, do you want to go see Cinderella a week on Saturday?'

I was glad no one would lend me their bikes. Besides riding round these basins you had to do all sorts of tricks like standing up on the saddle and doing the bucking bronco—pulling the bike up in the air by the handlebars and bouncing the front wheel up and down as you went round and that. If you didn't, well you were yellow.

'Pity I can't get anybody's bike off them,' I said to Marion. 'I could show you how to do a bucking bronco.'

'Seen it,' said Marion. 'Seen some lads out of the Catholic school do it.'

'Maybe so, but not blindfolded.'

We stood and watched them for a bit, Mono pulling his bike up out of the first basin and dipping down into the second one, then coming back and going round no hands. He was good. We thought he was going to come off. Every time he came round I shouted: 'Lend us your bike, Mono! Go on! Give you it back!'—knowing all the time that he wouldn't lend us it. Mono rode on to the second basin and then on to the third. Marion and me stayed where we were, started trying to skim slates over the dried-up mud at the bottom of the basin. Big Rayner was still messing about with Raymond Garnett. He was putting his knee in Garno's back and trying to get him down. Anyway, somehow or other Raymond Garnett gets away and starts running up the path. Big Rayner goes after him. I shouted: 'Go it, man!' and then went on skimming slates, because it was nothing fresh to see Raymond Garnett getting raced. Then I heard Big Rayner shout out: 'Mind out, Garno!' I looked up the path. Garno was pelting along looking round to see if Big Rayner was catching up with him, and he just missed running into this fellow who was coming towards us down the path past the fourth basin, riding his bicycle and sticking his leg out at the others. The man leaned over and went: 'Grr-*quack*!' at Garno, and everybody cracks out laughing.

I was standing near Ted by now. I forgot about our quarrel and grabbed hold of his sleeve. 'Hey, look man, there's that feller!' I shouted.

'*I* know, man, I'm not blind! Get o-o-off!'

'Hey, watch if he makes that noise!'

Ted went: 'Grr-qu-ack!' quietly so the man wouldn't hear, but not at me.

'Do it louder,' I said.

'Shu-u-ut up, man!' said Ted. Then he went: 'Grr-*qua*-ack!' He did it louder. The man was riding very slowly down the path, going so slow that he had to keep steering his front wheel about to keep from falling. All the others were standing round watching him.

'Hey, that feller yesterday afternoon! In our street! Where he hit your stick!' I said.

'Grrrr-*qu-ack*!' went Ted, but he wasn't talking to

me, he was talking to Mono and Little Rayner and anyone else who would listen.

I turned back to Marion. 'Saw that feller in our street yesterday,' I said.

The man was nearly up to the first basin now. Mono was riding just behind him, mocking him, and all the others were laughing at Mono and trying to push each other under his bike wheels. Little Rayner, Big Rayner's brother, starts walking kay-legged right at the side of this man's bicycle and singing 'Away in a manger' at him. He was dead cheeky.

The man was right up to us now. Don't ask me why, but Ted and me suddenly got right shy. Ted starts trying to shove Raymond Garnett down into the basin, and I pretended to be blind in my left eye and turned so that he could see my closed eye as he went past.

He still had this mucky old blazer on, and even from where I was standing you could see the hair sprouting out of his ears. His bike was an old sit-up-and-beg with bits out of the mudguards. He could ride it, though. He came right to the edge of the basins, sticking his leg out and winking at everybody and going: 'Grr-qua-ack! Grr-qu-a-*ack*!' Then all of a sudden he takes a Shirley Temple lollipop out of his pocket and starts riding round the basin, holding it up so that everybody runs round after him.

Shirley Temple lollipops were right dear. You couldn't buy them just out of a shop. You had to have twelve wrappers off a Licorice Chew and then you took them to Garnett's shop and they gave you a Shirley Temple for them. These wrappers were like money. They were all crinkly and you used to smooth them out and put them in your stocking top. Well, this man must have bought twelve sticks of Licorice Chew to get that lollipop.

Anyway, he goes round and round the basin holding this lollipop out, and all the kids started running after him, grabbing for it. They were all shouting: 'Give us it! *Will* yer?' Then he would start pretending to eat it and they would all shout out: 'Aw, *give* us it!'

He kept holding the Shirley Temple higher and higher, making them jump for it. Then he would pretend to throw it, like you do with a dog, and they would all run after it. All this time he was going round and round on his bike, going: 'Grr-qua-ack!' He was blinking crackers. Then at last he dropped it. I don't think he meant to drop it. A little lad with ginger hair was first there and he picked it up and ran in the direction of me and Marion. I didn't know him. He must have gone to the Catholic school.

I said: 'What's he given you?'

The ginger-haired kid said: '*No*thing.'

I said: '*He* has, man, it's a Shirley Temple. Let's have a look"

The kid said: '*It's* nothing,' and ran away. I shouted after him: '*I'll* tell, don't *you* worry!' but he was gone. So was this man as well. He was cycling off down the path and they were all running after him shouting: 'Give us one. Go on, mister! Give us one!' I shouted: 'Lend us your bike, mister!' after him, but it was a high-pitched shout that the man wasn't supposed to hear.

Mono had come off his bike in the bottom of the basin. I said: 'Hey, what do they call that feller?'

'Charlie Peace, what do you think they call him?' said Mono. Then Little Rayner comes up, all out of breath where he'd been chasing this man. I said: 'What do they call that feller, Rayno?' Little Rayner was a thief. He was in 3B. He used to go through people's coats in the cloakroom.

'*I* don't know. They call him Uncle Mad,' said Little Rayner.

'Who says they do?'

'They do. *I* don't know.'

'He's crackers, is that feller,' said Mono.

'Hey, he went down to Edmondson's for some chips,' said Raymond Garnett. 'Says have you got any chips left. So she says yer. So he says serves you right, shouldn't have cooked so many.'

'*He-e-e* didn't,' said Big Rayner. He was the biggest kid of the lot. He was years older than the rest of us. He had only one more term to go, then he would be leaving school. He was in the boy sprouts. He used to swear. 'Did he Joe buggery,' said Big Rayner.

'Did,' said Raymond Garnett. Raymond Garnett told lies. He always wore shoes instead of boots. He was like a blinking girl. He was always getting hit by Big Rayner. His father kept that shop at the top of our street. 'Serves you right, shouldn't have cooked so many,' he said again. 'Hey, he comes into our shop and says have you got any Wild Woodbines. So my mother says yer. So he says well tame 'em. *O*mmi! Get o-o-o-off! *O*mmi!' went Raymond Garnett.

'What do they call him Uncle Mad for?' asked Ted.

''Cos he's crackers,' said Mono. 'What do you think for?'

I was still pretending to be blind in my left eye. I screwed it up tight and looked down the path with my other eye, but Uncle Mad was out of sight.

'Have we to go after him?' I said.

'What for, see where he's gone?' said Mono.

'Yer.'

Thought Ted might come with me, but all he said was: 'Barmpot thinks he can catch up with a blinking bike.'

I said: '*I'm* off, any road.' I started off down the path with Mono shouting after me: 'He'll get you!'

Marion had vanished, so I went on my own. I pelted down to the cinder path and up Carnegie Road. I saw a little girl playing hopscotch by herself; thought that was her but it wasn't. 'Have you seen a man on a bicycle going past here?' I said. She thought I was a detective. She said: 'No who?' I said: 'Never mind who, just watch out for him and report to us. I only wish I had my full sight then I'd have got him myself by now.' She didn't notice that I was blind in one eye.

I wondered whether to go back to the basins or else go home for a cup of water. I thought about having to go back up the path saying: 'Lost track of him,' and Ted going: 'Could have told him that before he set off,' and I thought I'd go home instead. I went along Carnegie Road and up Royal Park Crescent into our street. I was hoping my Auntie Betty was out so that I could take a penny out of the gas money in the cupboard and look at the insurance books in the sideboard. Nothing *else* to blinking do. Then I heard somebody shouting: 'Wait on!' and saw Marion running up Coronation Grove after me.

She caught up with me and said: 'Are you going up our street?'

I said: 'Well I'm not going down it, am I?' and we walked up Coronation Grove together.

3

AFTER that, me and Marion started doing all sorts together. We built a little garden up at the top of their yard and put a border of half-bricks round it. We planted poppies in it and poured cupfuls of water in to make them grow. We went collecting tram tickets and added up the numbers to see what our fortunes were. One for sorrow, two for joy, three for a letter, four for a boy. I was a three. What you had to do, you had to add up all the figures on the tram ticket together and see what they came to, then divide by seven and see what's left over. Marion showed me how to do that. She knew a lot, did Marion. It was her that told me that if you swallow chewing gum, well it gets all tangled up round your heart, and if you swallow orange pips, well you get oranges growing out of your ears.

We started going into their house as well, making jigsaws up out of old pictures, but not when her mother was in, though. Her mother used to say Marion hadn't to play with me, only she worked most of the time, she used to clean our classrooms out every night, so she was never in. Mr Longbottom was always in, though. He was all right, even if Mrs Longbottom wasn't. He used to be always cracking jokes and that. Used to go: 'Do kippers swim folded or flat?' Used to be always telling us there were some treacle mines down near Parkside tram stop, and when we came back from getting tram tickets he would say: 'Have you found them treacle mines yet?' And he used to tell you riddles: 'What goes up but can't come down? Smoke.' He could speak in foreign as well. He used to fetch bits of metal home from work for us.

I know Ted didn't like him, though. He used to think he was making fun of us. Just because he used to go: 'How long is a piece of string?' and Ted couldn't answer. It was different when Ted used to ask *you* riddles, though.

Ted used to come and stand at Longbottom's gate with the other kids whenever Mr Longbottom stood telling riddles, but I wasn't getting back on pals with him, though. We still used to walk past each other without speaking, and he was going about with Mono and Big Rayner and them, so I didn't bother. Needn't think *I* was going to speak first, for a start. Thought I might as well leave it till I had to go to the pantomime with him and his mother next Saturday. So what I used to do, I went round with Raymond Garnett for a bit, only he was such a blinking swankpot that I used to spend most of my time with Marion.

I wasn't bothered, but I don't say I didn't feel a bit out of it when I used to see all the other kids disappearing into Clarkson's woods and I couldn't go with them because of Ted.

Like that day I had to go to the Co-op for my Auntie Betty, and I saw all the others going off somewhere and didn't know where they were going.

I used to hate going to the Co-op. It was miles away right up at the top of Parkside. It smelt of bacon and sawdust and there was always a right big queue, and I could never remember our Co-op number. Always used to say four-nine-two-nought-six instead of four-nought-two-nine-six or whatever it was, then I would get played pop with for taking the Co-op check home with the wrong number on it.

There was only one good thing about going to the Co-op and that was the red notebook with the Danger Don'ts on the back that my Aunt Betty used to write the orders down in. She wrote everything down on a fresh page every week, and the Co-op man, he used to cross each thing out as he put it in the basket. Then he would tear off a piece of that paper that they put yeast in and wrap the change up in it. Never gave *me* anything, though. Anyway, what I used to do with this notebook, every week I used to pinch four blank pages out of the middle. My Auntie never used to notice it was getting thinner all the time. I used to make magazines up out of this paper and give them to people.

Anyway, this day that I'm talking about, Marion Longbottom had to go to the Co-op as well, so I thought she might as well come with me. When we got up to the top of our street we see Mono and Big Rayner and them, just setting off down Coronation Grove. They were with Barbara Monoghan, she was Mono's sister, and Kathleen Fawcett. They were both dirty. They were always lifting their clothes up and picking their noses and that. Not like Marion. If her clothes crept up by accident when she was skipping or playing piesball she would always say: 'Oo, I'm showing next Monday's washing' and pull them back down again.

Anyway, get to the top of our street and Mono and Big Rayner start staring at us and nudging each other.

Barbara Monoghan says something to Kathleen Fawcett, and they both crack out laughing.

'What's up with them, stare-bears?' says Marion.

I said: 'Aw, you don't want to take any notice of them.' We turned into Parkside and walked on towards the Co-op. It was a hot day, hotter than it had been all summer, and once Big Rayner and them were out of the way, it was very quiet. I wondered where they were all going.

As we walked on I got Marion to hold my Auntie Betty's shopping basket while I opened the order book, raised up the staples in the middle, took a double page out and smoothed the staples down again so that nobody could tell. I put the clean sheet of paper in my pocket.

'What are you going to do with that?' said Marion.

'I make magazines up,' I said. 'Haven't you ever seen the Coronation Grove Gazette?'

'No, why, do you write it?'

'Yer. It comes out every month.' What I used to do, I used to cut things out of the paper and stick them in, then I'd make up one or two puzzles and then pass the Coronation Grove Gazette round for people to read.

'I like them film books best,' said Marion.

'I'm off to *make* a film book,' I said. 'I'm off to call it the Weekly Film Gazette. Do you want to read it?'

'Why, is it finished?'

'No, but it will be soon.' I hadn't even started it yet. 'I'll give you it when it is.'

'Well don't give anybody else it first,' said Marion. I thought I'd start on it as soon as I got back home. If I pinched another four pages out of the order book I could make it a special bumper number.

Anyway, it takes us an hour to get all these rotten groceries, then we set off back. It was even hotter when we came out of the Co-op; there were no kids playing round the doorway like there usually were and I wondered if there was a new game on somewhere and nobody had told us. We walked on, and when we get back to the top of our street we see Raymond Garnett, just coming out of their shop. First kid we'd clapped eyes on for ages.

'Coming down our street, man?' he said.

'Why, where you going?' I said.

'*I* don't know,' he said. 'Can go to the house shop if you like, if there's just us two. I've got threepence.'

He used to say things like that to make you go out with him. I knew he wasn't going near the blinking house shop, and even if he did, he wouldn't give me anything.

I mumbled: 'Be seeing you' at Marion, and walked off with Raymond Garnett. Took the groceries in and put them on the draining board, then we set off for the house shop. It was this house round in Royal Park Crescent where she used to sell stuff out of a drawer. I thought I might as well go with Raymond Garnett and see how far we got before he remembered he had to spend his threepence on something else.

We had just got to the bottom of our street when he stops and clasps his hand to his forehead.

'Oh, just remembered. My mother said I could only have threepence if I spent it at our shop.' Just like him.

'Have we to go up to your shop, then?' I said.

'Can't, man. It's closed.' Thought as much.

We stood there looking dateless for a minute or

two. The street was hot and stuffy and dark, sort of. It wasn't actually *dark* but the light was a glassy sort of light. You felt you were closed up in a sort of glass case and nothing—the houses, the lamp posts, the grates, the dead hopscotch marks—looked real. They looked like our school when you went past it during the holidays.

'Wonder where the others have gone?' I said.

'Don't know, have we to go round to the tusky fields and see if they're there?' We used to call rhubarb tusky. The rhubarb fields were in between the back of Coronation Grove and Clarkson's woods.

'Might as well,' I said.

We started walking back up Coronation Grove. It was right hot. We were just going to cross to go through Theaker's garden when I saw Marion, sitting on their gate. She must have only just come out again after taking the groceries in. She was chalking round the number plate on the gate post with a piece of brown sandstone. There was no one else in sight. She had no one to play with.

'Look as though we haven't seen her,' said Garno.

We walked past Marion without speaking to her. I started limping. I wanted to make her sorry. She didn't take any notice, and neither did we.

Just as we went past Fawcett's we saw Kathleen Fawcett coming out of their garden. She looked as though she'd been somewhere and was on her way back. She must have just been to their house for a cup of water.

We didn't take any notice of her, but Marion called out: 'Where are you going, Kathleen?'

'There and back to see how far it is, where do you

think I'm going?' said Kathleen. She was nasty. She was always having her head shaved.

'Yer, well my mother says I haven't to play with you,' said Marion. 'So you know.' As a rule she spoke properly, but when Kathleen or Barbara Monoghan were on to her, she spoke like they did all sneering.

'Nyah nyah nyah nyah nyah!' chanted Kathleen, taking Marion off but without using words. She pushed her body forward and pulled her tongue out.

'Have you seen all?' called Marion.

'Oo, have you seen all?' mimicked Kathleen. Marion shouted: 'You wait!' and Kathleen said: 'Go on home, your mother wants your boots for loaftins.'

'Nyah nyah nyah nyah nyah!' imitated Marion.

Kathleen turned her back and pulled her dress up at Marion. Then she went through Theaker's garden towards the rhubarb fields.

'You just wait!' Marion called after her.

The street was quiet again. Me and Garno stood in Coronation Grove to give Kathleen Fawcett chance to get through Theaker's, and we looked up and down the street. It was too quiet. I could just hear a motor bike going along Parkside. You couldn't hear anything else. I used to have this dream where my mother was beckoning me from the other side of a field, and no matter how far I ran she was still the same distance away. It was like that. It made me feel sad like you get back from church on Sunday nights and the house is all quiet with reading.

Right at the top of the street I had noticed a kid walking down towards us, and now he was getting nearer. He had one of his legs in irons. I wished I'd got an iron on my leg as well. We didn't know him, but he was singing to himself. He was singing some words to this hymn, and they sounded strange and distant.

There is a happy land, far far away
Where they have jam and bread three times a day.
Just one big fam-i-lee,
Eggs and bacon they don't see,

I had never heard these words before, and I had never seen the kid who was singing them. They sounded ghostly and mournful, and even though it was hot I shivered as he sang the last lines with a strange sad lilt:

Get no sugar in their tea,
Three times a day.

The kid walked past us without speaking, without even looking at us, and limped off down Coronation Grove.

Marion had finished chalking round their number plate and now she was covering the top of the gatepost with chalk.

'Are you coming to the tusky fields?' I shouted.

'*You're* not asking her, are you, man?' whispered Raymond Garnett.

'Might as well,' I said.

Marion jumped down off the gate. 'Not bothered,' she said. She ran across the road to meet us. Garno just went: 'Tt!' We all left the empty street together, going through Theaker's garden. We could see Kathleen Fawcett climbing the fence at the far side of the field.

'Have we to go to the clearing and do a play?' said Marion. The clearing was like a flat grass hill in

Clarkson's woods. There was a tree that we used to climb and some bushes with a cave through. We used to give plays there.

'Yer, there might be some of the others there,' said Garno.

We set off over the rhubarb fields, pushing the heavy green leaves aside where they came up to our waists. It was still very quiet, and the fields looked bigger than usual. We crossed through the Clerk of Works' department and into Clarkson's woods. We got as far as the basins, but there was nobody there. We heard a voice, a long way off like a motor bike, shouting: '*All in, all in, where e-ver you are!*' But it came from the far end of the woods, and we knew it was no one in our street.

The woods, as well, looked bigger. The grass was very green. The trees seemed more spaced out than usual. Our feet made loud squishing noises through the ferns.

We reached the clearing, and there was nobody there either. I shouted: '*All in, all in, where e-ver you are!* but nobody answered.

It was very dark in the woods, and very still.

'*Be* drunk,' said Marion. I used to play at being drunk, going: 'Yo bo yo bo yo' all over the shop. I did it now, but neither of them took any notice. Garno was swinging from the lowest branch of the climbing tree, about a foot off the ground. Couldn't have got any higher even if he'd wanted to, he couldn't climb. Marion sat on the edge of the clearing. I came and sat with her. She started looking for dandelion clocks but there were none, only the bright yellow dandelions.

'One o'clock, two o'clock, three o'clock,' she went. She picked one or two dandelions.

'They'll make you pee the be-ed!' I said. She dropped them. I got up and started pulling Garno's legs where he was swinging.

'You-ou'll tear my blinking trousers, man!' he shouted, and jumps down. He was always frightened of ripping his blinking clothes. All his clothes looked like best suits. Don't know why he ever came out at all. I shouted: '*All in, all in, where e-ver you are!*' again, and Garno puts his hand to his mouth and tries to do a Red Indian yodel. He couldn't do it for toffee, he never could, and there was no reply except from the echo. We had never noticed an echo in Clarkson's woods before.

'Lend us your glasses, Raymond,' said Marion.

'Can't, I've got to keep them on,' he said. He took his glasses off and breathed on them, then rubbed them on his sleeve. He put them back at the end of his nose and starts strutting with his hands together like a parson. Barmpot.

I went: 'That feller!' and started imitating this Uncle Mad, but neither of them seemed to know what I was on about. So I went: 'No, this is it!' and started walking right fast round the clearing with my knees bent and my finger wagging in front of my nose. It was supposed to be an imitation of the Marx Brothers that Ted used to do sometimes. Marion said: 'Be drunk. *Go* on.'

There seemed to be no one else in the woods at all except us.

We sat picking grass for a bit, then I think all three of us at once got that feeling that you get when you have all your toys out on the floor, all the big toys like the fort and the garage and the model theatre, then suddenly you want to be outside under the lamp post, playing hiddy with the others.

Garno suddenly said: 'Let's go pinching staples out of the Clerk of Works!' He jumps up and set off running down the bank of the clearing and I followed after him. Marion screamed: '*I'm* not going, so you needn't think I am!' but she ran after us and soon she called out: 'Wait on!'

The Clerk of Works' department was a big yard where they kept all the stuff for repairing this housing estate where we lived. There was a big flat-roofed garage that you had to muscle across, hanging three feet off the ground and travelling across the guttering with the tips of your fingers. There was all sorts inside this yard. Wood. Lead. Nails. Rope. All sorts. And these big sacks of staples. There were millions of them. We used to pinch these staples in pocketfulls. They were all over Coronation Grove nearly every night.

We get to the Clerk of Works, and Marion wouldn't come in, and I didn't think Raymond Garnett would either. He was always scared stiff whenever we were going anywhere where you weren't supposed to go. He used to wait outside and say he was seeing if there was anybody coming. Anyway, he couldn't do that tonight because Marion was waiting outside instead.

Marion stood outside the yard and kept shouting: 'The feller's coming!' in a hoarse whisper as we climbed in, but we knew he wasn't. We got over the barbed wire and jumped into the yard.

We didn't like it in the yard either. It seemed somehow as if everybody had run away and hidden.

Everything was covered with tarpaulin. We ran our fingers through the rich cream of staples standing in an open stack. I began to fill my pockets. Raymond Garnett wouldn't. He daren't. He was scared stiff that he would get stopped with some on him. I got my pockets so full that my coat began to sag under the weight, and then I didn't want them and I began to shovel them out again. I didn't want them. I stared at a hut that was labelled 'Time Office.' I read the sign over and over again until it looked stupid. There was nothing to do in the Clerk of Works and I wished we hadn't come.

From outside Marion called: 'There's the feller. There *is*!' I shouted back: '*Shu-ut* up!' but Marion, her voice growing squeaky and excited called in a shout-whisper: 'There's the feller, get hiddy!' and we knew it was true. So of course, Raymond Garnett starts dancing about like a cat on hot bricks. He was nearly blinking roaring. 'It was you that wanted to come if he gets us!' he went. I said: '*Shu-ut* up, screwy!'

We lay flat on our stomachs at the side of this big pile of planks. Soon we heard the thick crunch of boots on the cinder path that led past the Clerk of Works from Royal Park Crescent. We lay quite still, and I could hear Raymond Garnett starting to cry to himself like a blinking baby.

The planks were right up against the wall. The sound of the boots came past us and faded. Marion called: 'It's all right, it's only a feller.' Raymond Garnett got up and said: 'Cuh, thought they'd got us that time!' I said: 'Come on!' and even though there was no one to catch us we ran out of the Clerk of Works department bent double like two hunchbacks.

Outside Garno said: 'I'm going home to read my *Radio Fun*.'

Marion said: 'So am I.'

I suddenly felt almost sick with loneliness. The air around us was still heavy and the night gave out nothing but these far-off motor-bike noises.

I said: 'Have we to go up to the den? Bet the others are up there.'

The den didn't really belong to us. It was in a field at the top end of the Clerk of Works department. It had been made out of planks pinched out of the Clerk of Works and put across each other, like dovetail. It had two floors, an upstairs and a downstairs. It was a smashing place. It belonged to the big lads up at the top of our street, Big Rayner and them, but they sometimes let us go in it.

'*I'm* not going,' said Garno.

'What's up, are you yellow?' I said. I tried to hide how much it meant to me that they should go.

'No, my mother wants me,' said Garno.

'Co-ome *on*. I'll lend you my theatre,' I said. I would have *given* him the blinking theatre. It was made out of Kellog's corn-flakes boxes and we used to give puppet shows out of it, three buttons a time.

'Well we'll go up to the den, but if there's no one there well we're not stopping,' said Marion.

'He's to lend us his theatre, then,' said Garno. Just like him. He already had one blinking theatre, a proper toy theatre with curtains and footlights and that, but he has to have mine as well.

'*All* right,' I said.

'Honest to God?'

'Yer-er-ss!'

'On your mother's deathbed?'

'*Yerss!*'

'Say on my mother's deathbed.'

'*O-on* my mother's blinking deathbed!'

We set off for the den. We walked round by the cinder track and crossed into the field where the den was. It wasn't a field really; it was just a patch of dirt. The dirt looked dry and dusty, and the den looked empty.

Garno said: '*Come* on, man, there's no one there.' He tracked off to go through the gardens into Coronation Grove.

I shouted: 'Wait a minute!' I had seen somebody crawling out of the entrance to the den. It was Ted. He straightened up and started doing the Red Indian yodel. He could do it properly, even if Raymond Garnett couldn't. We all started running towards him.

Ted shouted: '*All in, all in, where e-ver you are!*' The night was still grey but the grey had become as magic as bonfire night. We pelted off through the dusty field. Marion tripped and shouted: '*Wait* on!' but we weren't waiting for anybody. We reached the den and scrambled inside through the low opening in the criss-cross of planks. All the others were there, and it was like stepping out of a foggy Monday morning into a hot scullery smelling of new cake and dumplings.

4

W E hadn't been in the den for more than two minutes before we knew that we weren't wanted there.

It was dark when you got inside, but as my eyes got used to it I could see Mono sitting on his heels in the corner, drawing bubbly gum out of his mouth with his finger and pulling it back again. Big Rayner sat on the edge of the upper storey, dangling his legs over the opening where you have to heave yourself up.

All the others were there. Barbara Monoghan was kneeling down with Kathleen Fawcett. Ted had started lying on his back with his feet against the wall as if he were trying to climb up it, and making breathing noises. Little Rayner was up on the top floor, playing a tommy talker.

They all shut up when we came in.

Barbara Monoghan started first. She went: 'Oo, look what the cat's brought in!' at Marion. Marion took no notice of her.

'We've been all over, haven't we, man?' said Garno. I said: 'Yer.'

'Did you get raced off the tusky fields?' shouted Little Rayner from upstairs.

'No, did we heckers like,' I said. You weren't supposed to go in the rhubarb fields.

'*We* got raced, didn't we, Mono?' shouted Little Rayner.

'*Shu-ut* up, our kid, before I come up there and bray you!' went Big Rayner.

They all just sat round not saying anything. Me and Marion and Garno squatted down on one side of the wall, but you could tell they didn't want us. Ted started snoring as though he was asleep.

Then Kathleen Fawcett started going: 'I spy with my little eye, something beginning wi-ith——'

I could tell they hadn't been playing this before we came in. They'd been talking about something else, and they were just waiting for us to go.

'—"C" ' said Kathleen Fawcett.

'My coat,' said Marion.

'No.'

'Somebody's cap, then,' said Barbara Monoghan.

'*No-o!* There isn't any caps!'

'There is!'

'—n't.'

'Clerk of Works!' shouted Little Rayner from upstairs.

'Yer,' said Kathleen Fawcett.

'*You-ou* can't see the Clerk of Works from where you're sitting,' said Barbara Monoghan.

'Oh, can't I, well I can then, so you know!'

Big Rayner and Mono were keeping quiet. They were not joining in the game. They were just sitting there trying to look as though they hadn't been doing anything before we came in. I could tell. I thought they'd been smoking cinammon, but there was no smell of it. Then I noticed **Mono** trying to fasten the back of his braces where **they'd come** unfastened. He put on this stupid smirk and tried to look as if he was scratching his back when he saw me looking at him, though.

Little Rayner came to the opening on the upper floor. He was lying flat on his stomach and he put his hand over the edge of the opening, next to where Big Rayner was sitting.

'Ur, look what's come!' he said, looking at me. He was dead cheeky. He lolled his head over the opening and started spitting, slowly and on purpose, on the floor below. Ted started reciting: 'Scab and matter custard, green phlegm pie——' but only Raymond Garnett took any notice, going: 'Yerks, man!'

Suddenly Mono said: 'Caw, it's clap cold sitting here!'

Don't ask me why, but I knew straight away that he'd touched on whatever it was they were hiding from us. Big Rayner spurted out laughing: 'Kkkkksssssh!' So did Barbara Monoghan. Kathleen Fawcett looked down at the ground, trying to keep a straight face. Then she burst out laughing as well. I knew straight away that whatever had been going on it was something shared by Big Rayner, Mono, Kathleen Fawcett and Barbara Monoghan. It was nothing to do with Mono being clap cold but his words—maybe just even the fact that he had spoken at *all*—touched all four of them in some way.

It had nothing to do with Ted or Little Rayner.

I don't think Raymond Garnett noticed anything. He said: 'Hey, we've pinched a right lot of staples out of the Clerk of Works.'

'*Have* yer?' said Mono, seriously.

'Yer. Look.' Garno fished a staple out of his pocket.

He never pinched any staples. He must have found it sticking to his coat. Mono picked it up carefully and pretended to look at it as though he had never seen a staple before.

'We nearly got caught,' said Garno.

'Did you nearly get caught?' said Mono. He held the staple up and started looking at it with one eye closed and his mouth sticking out, as if he didn't know what it was. Garno saw that he was being mocked. Mono spluttered out laughing again.

Barbara Monoghan whispered something to Kathleen Fawcett and they started laughing too. Big Rayner turned to Marion.

'Where've you been, Marion?' he asked. His voice was mocking too.

'We've been pinching staples,' said Marion.

'Have you been pinching staples?' said Big Rayner, raising his voice as if he was surprised. '*Have* yer?'

'Yes,' said Marion. She didn't know they were having her on.

'Haven't you been in the tusky fields?' said Mono. Then all four of them start blinking spluttering again.

'We got raced out, didn't we, Mono?' shouted Little Rayner from upstairs.

'*You-ou* wasn't with us, our young 'un, so shut your gob,' said Big Rayner.

'Maybe not, but we came just after. Didn't we, Mono?'

'*I* don't know,' said Mono.

Little Rayner shut up. He started lolling his head over the opening upstairs again, dropping spit on to the ground below. Ted was keeping on snoring and looked like going on till somebody took any notice.

'Haven't you been in the tusky fields, Marion?' said Big Rayner.

'No, why?'

'Just wondered,' said Big Rayner. He started whistling the Dead March with his eyes lifted up towards the ceiling, like they do on the pictures. I was dead mad with him for having Marion on. 'Do they call you Long-bum?' he said. Marion pretended not to hear.

Barbara Monoghan and Kathleen Fawcett started whispering again.

'How old are you, Marion?' said Barbara.

'As old as my tongue and a bit older than my teeth, chanted Marion.

'She's the same age as me, cos she's in our class,' said Kathleen Fawcett. 'Aren't you, Marion?'

'What if I am?'

'Oo, what if I am?' mimicked Barbara Monoghan, baring her teeth.

'Just wondered, that's all,' said Kathleen Fawcett. They left Marion alone. Big Rayner and Mono started on me.

'Hiya, kid!' said Mono, winking at me.

I felt stupid but I had to wink back and go: 'Hiya!'

So Mono comes up close and starts staring in my face and going: 'What's up, man, have you got something in your eye?'

'No, course I haven't,' I said.

'What you winking for, then?' he said. 'You only wink when you've got something in your eye.' He tried to get hold of my eye and poke in it with his fingers. I struggled and he went: 'Let's have a look, man!' He came away holding his two fingers together and going: 'Oh, you'd have gone blind if I hadn't got this out.'

He went back and sat in the corner. He winked at Marion and said: 'Hiya, kid!' but she wasn't having any. He started staring at her, and she and Mono started staring each other out for a minute or two.

Then he starts on me and goes: 'Hey, do you go out with lasses, man?'

I couldn't say I didn't go out with lasses because they'd seen me come in with Marion.

'What if I do?' I said.

Mono sniggered. 'Ask him if he goes out with lasses,' he said to Big Rayner.

'Do you go out with lasses?' asked Big Rayner, trying to sound as though he really wanted to know.

'What for?' I said.

'Don't you *go* out with lasses?'

'He's the teacher's pet!' said Little Rayner, drooling his head over the upstairs opening. I would have shouted: 'I'll *bray* you!' if Big Rayner hadn't been there. Anyway, Big answered him himself.

'You shut your gob, our young 'un!' he said, pushing Little Rayner's head back. Then he turned back to me.

'Don't I want hold of you?' he said.

'No,' I muttered.

'Are you sure? Can't remember whether I want hold of him or not, can you, Mono?'

Mono pretended to look as though he was trying to remember. 'No. Wasn't it him that we brayed the other day?' Big Rayner was always braying somebody. He *might* have wanted hold of me for all I knew.

'Can't remember,' said Big Rayner. 'Anyway, we'll let him off this time.' I looked towards Marion to see if she was wondering why I didn't stick up for myself, but she was piling dust over her shoecaps and not bothering.

'Do you go out with Marion?' said Big Rayner.

'No,' I said, though I felt ashamed of myself for saying so. Marion looked up and said: 'I go out with myself.'

'Can *I* go out with her?' said Big Rayner, still looking at me.

I didn't say anything.

'Will you knock my block off if I go out with her?' jeered Big Rayner. Mono went: 'He'll murder you, man!' Big Rayner starts putting his hands up and going: 'Oh, don't hit me!' in a stupid, squeaking voice.

Barbara Monoghan joined in.

'Do you want to go out with Big Rayner, Marion?' she said.

'You get off her,' said Big Rayner. He thought he was good. 'She's all right, is Marion, aren't you, Marion?'

Barbara Monoghan whispered again to Kathleen Fawcett. My heart always started bumping when people whispered at each other. Kathleen starts giggling.

'What's our lass say?' said Mono.

'*No*thing, nosey,' said Barbara Monoghan.

'No, what's she say?' said Big Rayner.

'She says you're all right as well,' said Kathleen Fawcett very quickly so that the words rushed into each other. The two girls started giggling again. 'They must be crackers,' said Marion.

'Oh, must we?' sneered Barbara Monoghan.

'We know something about you, Marion Longbottom, don't we Barbara?' said Kathleen Fawcett.

'Yer, we do!' said Barbara. She didn't look as though she had any idea what Kathleen was talking about.

'*You* don't!' said Marion.

'*We* do!'

'Oh but you don't!'

'Oh but we do!'

Mono chimed in: '*We* saw you, Marion, didn't we, our lass?'

'Yer,' said Barbara.

'Saw me what?' said Marion, her face flushed with shame.

'*You* know,' said Mono.

They were all making it up as they went along. And all the time they were hiding something. I tried to stop them by shouting up at Little Rayner: 'Have you got any books to swop, Rayno?' but Mono sneered: '*Loo-ook* at 'em, trying to get out of it!'

He was trying to bring me into it now. They all shut up again, except for Barbara and Kathleen who kept giggling and pushing each other. Then Little Rayner started singing, like he always did when someone else was in trouble:

'There *was* a scotch high-lander
At the Battle of Wa-a-ter-er-loo——'

And he started making this noise like a drum, going: 'Brr-um pum-pum, brr-um pum-pum.' Suddenly Big Rayner said:

'Wouldn't like to be in your shoes, Marion!'

'Wouldn't like to be in yours, either,' said Marion.

'Wouldn't yer?' sneered Big Rayner.

'No, I wouldn't yer.'

'Why, what for?'

'*You* know what for.'

'What, just cos we were making fun of yer?' I saw that Big Rayner's manner had changed. He was giving these little short laughs. He was frightened about something.

'*I* know what you were doing in them tusky fields,' said Marion.

'What?'

'*You* know.'

'Know what you were doing that time as well,' said Big Rayner. 'So *you* needn't talk.'

I didn't know what either of them was talking about. Marion's face had gone white. Big Rayner still looked frightened.

'You don't want to go round calling people, Marion Longbottom, cos you might get something you don't want,' said Barbara Monoghan. Marion and Big Rayner said no more to each other. They only stared at each other, but you could tell that Big Rayner was no longer playing. Don't ask me why, but I suddenly wondered to myself whether he'd known Marion before she came to live in Coronation Grove. I knew for certain that whatever had been going on, Marion knew more about it than I did.

Little Rayner starts going: 'Wheezy Anna, swallowed a tanner, down where the water melons grow———'

Big Rayner jumped to his feet and got hold of their kid by his hair. 'If you don't shut up, our young 'un, you're going to get your sodding neck broke!' he shouted. Little Rayner shut up and crawled back to where nobody could get at him. Nobody said anything. Big Rayner stood there sniffing as though he'd just had a fight.

It seemed ages before I heard a woman's voice break into the quiet, shouting across the field: 'Ra-ay-ay-mond! *Ray*mond!'

'Your mother's shouting for you, Garno,' said Ted. Raymond Garnett tried to pretend he wasn't going, but Mono started going: 'Go on, Raymond, else mammy'll smack you, won't she?'

Raymond Garnett went and we all started moving as well, going in twos and threes through the gardens, some running, some walking. Marion shouted after Big Rayner: 'You just wait!' She was burning with hate and rage. I said: 'Never mind, Marion!' but she said it again: 'You just wait, Big Rayner!' in a quiet voice as though she were talking to me.

When we got into the street the others had started playing relieve-oh round the lamp post. I didn't want to play. Something had happened while the woods were so quiet that night and I knew it wasn't over. I started whistling to show that I hadn't done anything, and went in.

5

SHE was washing her feet in front of the fireplace when I got in, my Auntie Betty. The water looked grey and cold and it had a hard scum on it from the green soap she was using. The bowl had bits of black on the outside where the enamel was chipped off. The house was dark.

I never knew what to do when I found my Auntie Betty in and I always had to say something to prove I hadn't come in to take the gas money out of the cupboard or to pinch any sultanas off the breadboard. I used to come in from Sunday School and say: 'Hey, Mr Rich has started wearing glasses!' Mr Rich was the vicar at the Holy Cross church. We used to call it the Holy Hoss. He never wore glasses at all, really, but I told my Auntie Betty he did. Another time I went in and said our teacher's car had skidded up near Park Avenue, and it hadn't all the time.

Anyway, today I went in and said: 'Hey, Raymond Garnett's got a new cinematograph.'

My Auntie Betty was wiping her feet on a mucky old towel. She would never let you use an ordinary towel to dry your feet with. Always had to use this old grey one with holes all over it.

'Yes, well *you're* not having one,' my Auntie Betty said.

'Don't want one, I can borrow his if I want,' I said.

'You borrow nothing from nobody!' my Auntie Betty snapped. 'So you think on!'

'Don't *want* to borrow it, he only said I could if I wanted,' I said. 'Do you know who he got it off?'

'Somebody with more money than sense,' my Auntie Betty said.

She had started peeling her toenails all over the blinking rug. I couldn't stand watching her so I went to the cupboard and got the dominoes out. I sat down and tipped them out over the table.

'He got it off that feller,' I said.

'What feller?'

'Him that makes that noise,' I said. 'Him they call Uncle Mad.'

My Auntie Betty straightened up and stood on this mucky old towel at the side of the bowl. I saw straight away that it had gone too far and that she could easily find out I was lying.

'Well I *think* he did,' I said. 'Cos Raymond Garnett was in Clarkson's woods with it just after that feller left, and he didn't have it before that, I *do* know.'

'When were *you* in Clarkson's woods?' my Auntie Betty said.

'Just now. Might not be his cinematograph at all, though. He might have borrowed it.'

'And what have I told you about going in Clarkson's woods?' my Auntie Betty said.

Never expected her to carry on like that, else I'd never have started it. I started balancing my dominoes on top of each other and went: 'I-I-I only went in for a bit.'

'What have I *told* you about going in Clarkson's woods?'

'*W-e-e-ell!*' I went.

'I'll give you well! What were you doing there?'

'*We-e* were riding bikes!' I just had to make it up as I went along.

'Whose bikes?'

'*I* don't know. Ted's.'

'Well you don't go on Ted's bike or anybody else's bike. And you keep out of them woods. Do you hear?'

'*Y-e-e-es!*'

'Well think on!'

Had to shut up for a minute to let this pass. I started putting my dominoes in a long line and flicking them so that they fell down. My Auntie Betty is shuffling about on this old towel as if it was a doormat.

Then I remembered how this Uncle Mad had been dishing out lollipops that day when we *were* in Clarkson's woods, so I thought I might as well tell her about that, pretending it had only just happened.

I said: 'Nearly got a Shirley Temple given today, only another kid got it instead.'

So she starts again. 'Who gave him it?'

'That feller.'

'What feller?'

'Him on that bike. Him that you and Mrs Longbottom were talking about. Him that makes that noise!'

'Well you keep *out* of them woods! Do you hear? You go into the park in future, else you don't go out at all!' Her voice was getting right shrill.

'What's *up?*' I said.

'I'll give you what's up! And you keep away from that feller! And if he gives you anything you tell him you don't want it!'

'Gives us *what?*' The only reason I'd *men*tioned the

Shirley Temples was so that I could say that Uncle Mad couldn't have given Raymond Garnett his cinematograph after all, because he was on his bike and he couldn't have carried it, but I didn't get chance now. 'Gives us *what*?' I said.

'Anything at all. If he tries to give you any sweets. You don't take them.'

I was starting to feel right hot and prickly. I bent low over my dominoes, pretending to be looking for the double six.

'He goes into Edmondson's' I said, remembering Raymond Garnett's lie about Uncle Mad going into Edmondson's for some chips and saying they shouldn't have cooked so many.

'I'll Edmondson you if I see you talking to him,' my Auntie Betty said. 'You do as I say. And you don't go into them public lavatories in the park, neither.'

By now I was feeling right shy and a bit frightened, like that time I saw Mrs Fawcett letting their baby suck at her breast. I said: 'I don't *go* in them.' My Auntie Betty said: 'Well you keep out.'

She picked up the bowl of grey water and staggered through into the kitchen in her bare feet. It left a circle of wet on the rug, and as she walked it was spilling over the side on to the oilcloth.

From the kitchen she shouted: 'And who's been tearing pages out of that Co-op book?'

I didn't see why I should stop in now. I started putting my dominoes back in the box as fast as I could not even bothering to put them with all the spots showing. My Auntie Betty shouted: 'You don't go out again tonight! You get ready for bed!' I didn't know what was up with her.

I went and stood near the back door where I could slink out when she'd forgotten about it. I wondered what she'd say if she found out that Raymond Garnett hadn't got a cinematograph at all, then I thought what if somebody tells her I haven't even *seen* Uncle Mad today, and what if Big Rayner really wants hold of me like he said he did, and what if I get into cop it for being in the den with him and Mono and them, and how can I get out of going to the pantomime with Ted and his mother. My Auntie Betty started washing the bowl out under the tap, and after a bit I went into the back garden and started pretending it was a foreign country and I was the boss. Then after a while I got into my big hole at the top of the garden, and started digging.

6

JUST remembered, suppose I ought to tell you something about where we used to live. Well you know these big housing estates, well it was one of them. They were right wide streets with like big grass verges and that. We'd only lived there since just before I was born. It was all new, and even now they were still building bits on to it all over the shop. Down at the bottom of Parkside there were some new houses that no one had even moved into yet. We used to go down there on Saturday afternoons. There were splashes all over the walls where we'd been throwing mud-balls, and all the fences had footmarks where all the kids from the Catholic school had been seeing how high up they could kick.

It was like that all over the estate. There were big like greens all over with these little fences round, only most of the fences had been pulled up when we went chumping for bonfire night, and these greens had all paths worn across them where people had been taking short cuts.

Where I liked it best, though, was on the other side of the park, where the old fire engine was.

You had to crawl through like a big drain pipe at the edge of the pipe, it was an old sewer, I think, and where it brought you out was in a long road with houses that had been there for ages, made out of stone.

You were clean out of the estate then. You just had to walk up this road and there was a coal-mine there with a lot of slag heaps, and railway lines that went right over the street, so that lorries bumped when they went over them. The houses were all in long rows and made of black stone, and all the streets were just rough cobbles with sooty grass growing through them. Not like *our* blinking street.

We used to go there a lot. I had started the Coronation Grove Hiking Society; there was only me and Ted in it, and before we fell out we used to go on hikes to the other side of the park, through this drainpipe. We used to go on these slag heaps, getting old pram wheels that people had thrown away, and playing on this big second-hand fire engine that they had, standing on a patch of old concrete nearby. Then I used to put it in the Hiking Gazette.

There was nothing like this fire engine on *our* estate. It was a big Leyland. All the ladders and bells and that had been stripped off but there was still that like platform where the firemen used to sit. It had done 45,000 miles. It had been painted navy blue, but you could still tell it was a fire engine. I think they used to use it for lugging stuff up on to the slag heaps, but it had stood on this patch of concrete as long as *I* can remember. We used to play at fire engines on it. The fellow who used to mind the slag heaps, he didn't mind you playing on it, but if the railway police came up and found you on it, they used to take your name and address.

One night we were all up in Parkside, playing hiddy, just before I went to the cubs. Most of the others were off getting lead piping to melt down, but I was going to the cubs. Little Rayner was playing. I didn't like Little Rayner playing when I had it because he used to go for blinking miles and while you were out looking for him someone would come rushing out through somebody's garden and relieve the others. If you said anything to him he used to tell Big Rayner of you.

Tonight, even though I had shouted: '*Nommi avit!*' first, I was It. I had to catch the others. As per usual Little Rayner pelts off before anyone else, right down Parkside, so I thought I would catch him first.

I knew he would be *in* our school playground, be*hind* the park gates, or else in somebody's garden.

I chanted: 'Seventy five *eighty*, eight five *ninety*, ninety five *hund*red, *coming*, ready or not!' Then I set off down Parkside, looking in the gardens. I caught Raymond Garnett just inside our school gates and sent him back to the lamp post. I got Ted behind a privet hedge, and even though I tigged him we had to pretend we didn't know each other. Then I started looking for Little Rayner, and I was so long finding him that the others had started a hiddy game of their own while we were waiting.

It was blinking ages before Little Rayner comes pelting back down Parkside. I had just been looking in somebody's dustbin, where I had caught him hiding once before. I zigzagged across the street and caught him by the jersey just as he was trying to get past.

'Two four six eight ten. *You're* caught.'

'Ge-et o-o-off, man!' Little Rayner struggled to get himself free and shouted all in. Raymond Garnett came running up. Little Rayner was excited.

'Hey, you know that drainpipe?' he said.

'Yer.'

'Well you know them slag heaps?'

'Yer.'

'Well you know that fire engine?'

'Yer.'

'Well it's gone.'

The others had come up by now. They all started saying: '*You* lie!' and '*I-it* hasn't, man!' and '*I-it* doesn't go!'

Raymond Garnett said: 'Tell us something we don't know.'

'Well *you* didn't know it was gone!' said Little Rayner.

'Course I did!'

'Course you didn't!'

'Course I did! Knew before you did!'

'Who's bought it, Garno?' Ted asked Raymond Garnett.

'Him on the Quaker Oat box!' said Raymond Garnett. *He* didn't know who'd bought it.

'No, who's bought it, man?'

'Someonewhosenamebegins wi-i-th——' Raymond Garnett didn't know anything about it at all.

The hiddy game broke up with Ted and Little Rayner chasing Raymond Garnett up Parkside. The others set off pinching lead. I set off for the cubs.

Down Wharfedale Crescent I caught up with Raymond Garnett and walked with him towards the cub hut. He was a sixer, was Garno. Ted and Little Rayner had pulled his neckerchief out of his woggle and he was just fastening it up again.

'You want to see what I did to *them*, though,' he said. He hadn't touched them, if you ask me anything. Daren't for one thing.

We started walking down past Holy Hoss church, towards the cub hut. We were just turning into the cub hut when a kid down the road shouted: 'That ball, man!' There was this tennis ball in the road just near us. It had somebody's initials on it in copying ink. I went up and kicked it, only it went cock-eyed. It always did every time I kicked a ball. I couldn't kick.

Anyway, I ran over the road to kick the ball again, and that was how we saw this fire engine again. It was the same one. I didn't even know it could go. It was all piled up with logs and it had all mud and twigs round the tyres.

I shouted for Garno, and he came pelting up. I grabbed him by the arm and said: 'Hey, look man, there's that fire engine off them slag heaps!'

'I-I-I know, man, I'm not blinking blind!' said Garno. We walked up and looked at it. It looked even worse than it used to do standing outside the slag heaps. We started kicking the tyres.

'Off that fire engine!' someone shouted. We looked round and it was this kid whose ball I had kicked cockeyed. He was standing with two other kids in one of the gardens just opposite. I didn't know who *he* was, but I knew who *they* were. One of them was the little ginger-haired kid who got the Shirley Temple lollipop off Uncle Mad when we were up at the basins that day. The other was the lame kid with his leg in irons who we'd seen in Coronation Grove that day before we went to the den, when we didn't know where everybody else had gone. I think they must have all gone to the Catholic school.

The kid who had spoken was the tallest of the three. He seemed to be the boss.

I said: 'It's not yours, what's up with you?'

He said: 'No, and it's not yours either. You've to get off it, hasn't he, Peggo?'

They were standing in this garden, but you couldn't tell it was a garden, it was just a blinking flat patch of earth, that's all. Someone had plonked these purple irises all along the edge of the path, but they were all trampled down with people walking all over them. The gate had come off its hinges and it was propped up against the privet.

'Whose garden is it?' I asked the kid with his leg in irons, the kid they called Peggo.

'Not yours,' he said.

'Bet it's not yours, either, I said.

One of the other two, the little pale-faced ginger-haired kid, pipes up: 'It's Uncle Mad's, is this.' They called him Gin'er.

'Is this where Uncle Mad lives? God's honour?' I said.

'Yer, where do you think he lives?' said Gin'er.

'That's his fire engine as well,' said the tall kid. They called him Spenco.

I grabbed hold of Garno again. 'Hey, this is where that feller lives!' I said. 'It's *him* that's got that fire engine! Him that makes that noise!' I started going: 'Grr-qua-ack!' to imitate Uncle Mad.

'Tell us something we don't know,' said Garno.

'He doesn't make that noise now,' said young Gin'er. 'He goes cuit-cuit-cuit-cuit-cuit now.' He made a noise like somebody calling a blinking cat.

'And does he live *here*?' I said again. What I asked him for, the house looked empty. There were no curtains up at any of the windows, and the walls were all chalk where somebody had been chalking on them. But the front door was open, though.

'Yer. It's his house,' said Peggo.

'And does he let you go in his garden?'

'Course he does,' said Spenco, the tallest of the three.

'Can *we* come in?' I said.

'Can if we let you.'

'Well can we?'

'*I-if* you want.'

We'd been leaning up against the old fire engine that Uncle Mad had got off the slag heaps. It was parked with the front wheels on the pavement and the back wheels about a mile in the middle of the road. We went into the front garden and stared through the front door. It was wide open. We could just see some bare floorboards. Spenco said: 'Wait there' and walks in, cheeky as anything. He went into the kitchen at the back and came back out again carrying this piece of rag. Uncle Mad followed after him, holding a bowl of water. He walked slowly so he wouldn't spill any. Even then, the water slopped over all the time and made little puddles all over the floor. It reminded me of my Auntie Betty washing her feet.

We got off the doorstep to let him come past. 'Uncle *Ma*-ad!' called Raymond Garnett.

Uncle Mad winked and made this new noise. 'Cuit cuit cuit cuit cuit!' like somebody calling the cat in. He walked past us and went up the path carrying his bowl of water.

Peggo, the kid with his leg in irons, was unscrewing the cap on the bonnet of the fire engine out in the road. Uncle Mad awkwardly tipped in the bowl of water. Most of it went on the road. Spenco started going over the bonnet with this piece of rag. Young Gin'er was just watching them. He was only a little titchy kid.

'Where did you get the fire engine, mister?' I shouted.

'Cuit cuit cuit cuit cuit!' went Uncle Mad.

'Bet he got it off them slag heaps,' I said to Raymond Garnett. I shouted: 'Bet you got it off them slag heaps, didn't you?'

'Cuit cuit cuit cuit cuit!'

Young Gin'er started going: 'Fire engine, bire engine, tire engine, sire engine, lire engine.'

I shouted: '*You* did! Didn't you, Uncle Mad?'

'Grr-*qua-ack*!' He made his old noise again.

'No, didn't you?'

'Grr-quack-qua-ack!'

'Pire engine, dire engine, mire engine,' went young Gin'er.

'I bet he did,' I said.

'He-e *did*n't, man,' said Spenco.

'Where *did* he get it, then?' I said.

'He didn't get it off them slag heaps, I can tell you that much,' said Spenco. They all started knocking twigs off the side of the fire engine. There were a lot of logs in the garden. They must have been out getting wood.

'We're all off getting stones out of Parkside quarries now,' said young Gin'er.

'Are you going on that?' I asked, nodding towards the fire engine. It didn't look as though it would reach the end of the street.

'Yer, what do you think we're going on?'

'Can *we* come?' I asked.

'*We're* not stopping you!' said Spenco.

Garno said in a whisper: 'Hey, what about the cubs, man?'

I said: 'You can go. I off getting stones.'

'We won't half get into cop it,' Garno said.

Uncle Mad came back into the garden. He put the bowl on the front doorstep. Doesn't bother to shut the door, just leaves it open. He went back to the fire engine and climbed into the driver's seat.

The three kids clambered up and sat on one side where the firemen used to sit. Peggo couldn't half climb, even if he *did* have his leg in irons. Me and Garno got up on the other side.

'Will he say anything to us for coming?' I shouted across to Spenco.

'No-o, course he won't. They can come, can't they, Uncle Mad?'

'Cuit cuit cuit!' went Uncle Mad.

'Haven't if we don't want to,' I said.

We set off up Wharfedale Gardens. Young Gin'er climbed up in front and started pretending to steer, going 'Brr-m, brr-m, brr-UM' as if he was the engine. Uncle Mad couldn't half drive. We turned into Wharfedale Avenue.

Little Rayner, the only one besides us who hadn't gone pinching lead, was walking up to the cub hut with some of the other cubs. He had only just joined. He started pointing up at the fire engine and shouting. I was glad we were on it and not him. I shouted: 'We're off getting stones!'

'*Don't* tell them, man!' said Garno. Then the next person we see is Akela, coming down the street, wearing a scout hat and a raincoat. I could tell he's seen us, so I thought I might as well salute. You weren't supposed to salute sitting down so I tried to get up, using Garno's shoulder to help me. The fire engine lurched and I got chucked down, sprawling all over Garno. I struggled up on to my knees and put two fingers up in this stupid salute. My cap was all lop-sided and I must have looked blinking barmy. Garno just sat there, putting on this sickly grin. Akela frowned and beckoned to us and pointed at the ground. He wanted us to get off. We just kept on grinning at him as if we were having our school photos taken.

'We're off getting stones, Akela! Aren't we, Uncle Mad?' I shouted. Uncle Mad made no sign, and Akela walked on.

We turned down Carnegie Road, and into Park Avenue, towards the quarries.

7

PARKSIDE quarries were over at the side of the park. Near Royal Park Woods. There were two of these quarries, a big one and a little one. There used to be all men working in them but they'd stopped now. There were blackberry bushes growing out of the side. We used to go blackbegging there.

They were both very deep, even the little one. It wasn't little really, but the other one was a bit deeper, so we used to call them the big one and the little one. Well the little one went down in a gradual slope all the way round, but this big one, well it went down like a blinking cliff edge on one side. Well these stones were at the bottom of *that*.

You couldn't climb down the cliff side. You had to go right round by the other end and slither down that way.

Uncle Mad stopped the fire engine right at the side of the big quarry and we all piled out.

'Not them little stones, only them big ones!' called Spenco. He thought he was the boss, but he wasn't.

'What does he do with them?' I asked.

'Who, Uncle Mad? He takes them home,' said Peggo.

We slithered down the side of the quarry and started picking up one of the big square stones each and staggering back up again. Peggo was too lame to come down. He stood at the top, helping us up on to the grass. Uncle Mad didn't come down either. He stood at the side of the fire engine, and when we brought the stones along he pushed them into position along the ledge where you sit.

'Does he give you anything?' I asked Spenco.

'He once gave me threepence,' Spenco said.

'What for, taking these stones up?'

'No, he just *gave* us it.'

We took up about twenty stones. Some of them were half buried in the ground at the bottom of the quarry and when you prized them up they had all sludge underneath.

Young Gin'er wasn't doing much. He didn't look strong enough to carry the big stones. He kept running up and down the sloping end of the quarry, holding his arms out like an aeroplane and going:'Nnnnnnnnnn!' all the time. Every time he got to the top he ran all the way round the quarry, going: 'Nnnnnnnnnn!' and when he passed Uncle Mad, Uncle Mad went: 'Grrr-*qua*-ack!'

All this time we were humping these big stones up. Spenco and Peggo shouted: '*Co-ome* on, man!' once or twice but young Gin'er took no notice. I didn't blame him.

Me and Garno gradually worked our way up towards the cliff side of the quarry. The other kids stayed at the other end. We got right up at the back of some blackberry bushes so we could have a rest.

'Fagged out,' said Garno. We sat down, and started looking up at the side of the quarry. I knew what Garno was thinking. He was thinking who could climb it. *He* couldn't for one, I knew that much. After a bit he nudged me and said: 'Dare you to climb down there.'

Thought so.

I looked up at the cliff side of the quarry. It was a sheer drop for miles all the way down.

'No fear,' I said. You could hardly *see* the top.

'Yar, you're yellow,' said Garno. 'There's only two can climb down there, me and Big Rayner.'

'Cur, let's see you do it, then,' I said.

'I've *done* it,' said Garno.

'*I* bet,' I said.

There was only one way you could get down the cliff side of the quarry, and that was by working your way down backwards using bits of stone and that as footholds. *Garno* had never climbed down it, but I wouldn't have been surprised if Big Rayner had.

'What's up, can't you *climb* down that side?' sneered Garno.

'Climb down as far as *you*,' I said.

'Well come on then.'

'All right, I *will* do.'

We got up and picked up a stone each and got round to the other side of the quarry where Uncle Mad was standing. I wasn't bothered about starting to climb down, because I thought he'd stop us. We dumped the stones and went and looked over the edge of the quarry. It was miles down to the bottom.

I wiped my hands down my cub jersey and got down backwards on my hands and knees and started feeling down the side of the quarry with my foot. Garno was still standing at the top like a blinking girl.

'What you waiting for?' I said.

'Just getting my breath back,' he said. 'Won't be a minute.'

I reached down with my foot and found like a branch growing out of the side of the quarry. I tested it and lowered myself down till I was standing on it, holding the edge of the quarry with my hands.

'Got *so* far,' I said. Garno still hadn't started, never would do, either. Uncle Mad was standing over by the fire engine. He wasn't even *looking* at me, never mind stopping me from going down. He was looking towards Royal Park Woods.

'Aren't you *going* any further?' said Garno.

'What's up with you, you can't get as far as *this*,' I said. Garno put on this stupid face, trying to look surprised.

'Aw, you don't think *I'm* going down, do you?' he said. He'd just been having me on. He said he could do it, but he couldn't all the time. Might have known.

I looked down the side of the quarry. It looked even deeper from where I was standing. I couldn't see how I could get down any further, so I thought I might as well climb back up again, seeing Garno wasn't coming down.

I could just see over the edge of the quarry. I started to heave myself up. Then Garno, blinking fool, he starts pretending to stamp on my hands.

'G-i-ive o-ver, barmpot!' I shouted.

Garno started laughing. 'Isn't half a big drop,' he said. 'Have I to fetch the ambulance?'

He drove his heel into the ground about an inch from where my hand was. I pulled my hand away and grabbed at the side of the quarry to stop myself from falling. It was all clay and I dug my fingers in it to get a good hold. A big chunk of it fell out and went rattling away to the bottom of the quarry. I shouted: 'I'm slipping, man! Get hold of my blinking hand!'

Garno suddenly saw that I wasn't acting and got hold of my arm and tried to pull me up but he couldn't. He shouted: 'Uncle Mad! He's slipping!'

Next thing I knew was Uncle Mad came rushing up and got hold of my arm and yanked me clean up and over the edge of the quarry. He picked me up and held me in the air, his hands under my arm-pits. He didn't say a word, he just went: 'Cuit cuit cuit cuit cuit!' like he did when we were all standing in his garden.

I went: 'Phew, thought I was a dead duck that time!' and waited for Uncle Mad to put me down. But he didn't, he just held me there. I suddenly began to feel daft and struggled to the ground. I didn't like him holding me up. I was right close to his face and could smell his breath and see this hair growing out of his ears and out of his nose as well.

I had got all sand and clay all over the front of my cub jersey and on my trousers. Garno tried to dash it off but it wouldn't all come. Uncle Mad stood looking at us for a bit, then he walked back to the fire engine.

'What have I to tell my Auntie Betty?' I said.

'Tell her you fell,' said Garno. I drew a deep breath and we set off back to the other side of the quarry. The other kids were still getting stones.

'Bet *you* were frightened, thingy!' shouted young Gin'er. We slithered down and started looking for these big stones. Young Gin'er started playing at aeros again.

74

After a bit he stopped and stood at the edge of the quarry and started looking out towards the park. He put his fists to his eyes, pretending they were binoculars.

Suddenly young Gin'er shouts down: 'Hey, thingy! Is them *your* cubs that's coming?'

I was just carrying a big stone up and resting at the side of a blackberry bush near the top. I let go of it and let it roll down, and scrambled up to the top of the quarry. Not far enough so anyone could see me, though. I whispered: 'Where, man?'

'*He-e's* kidding you, man!' shouted Garno from the bottom of the quarry.

'I'm not! You come and look!' said young Gin'er.

'Well what colour neckerchieves have they got?'

'Sky blue pink with yellow dots on.'

'No, what have they got?'

'Pale blue, same as yours.'

Garno crawled up the quarry and crouched down at the side of me. 'Bet they're tracking,' he said. 'Have we to get hiddy?'

'Behind this bush man!' I said. I said to young Gin'er: 'Tell us if they're coming this way.

'No, they're turning off,' said young Gin'er. 'There's a feller in a scout hat with them.'

Bet that was Akela. We crouched under the blackberry bush. After a bit young Gin'er called out: '*They've* gone!'

We got up and started climbing out of the quarry. Spenco and Peggo had stopped collecting stones and they looked as though they were getting ready to go home. Suddenly young Gin'er shouted: '*Back*, thingy! One of them cubs is coming!' But by that time we had clambered out on to the path leading round the quarry. Little Rayner, wearing a brand-new uniform, was coming towards us, and he saw us.

He shouted: '*We-e* know you're there, so you needn't hide!'

'Who's hiding?' shouted Garno. We went up to meet Little Rayner.

'Akela says you've to come,' he said as we reached him.

'What for, does he know we're here?'

'Yer, course he does. You aren't half going to get into cop it.'

Raymond Garnett went pale. I said: 'What are you all doing down in the park?'

'Going tracking. I'm going to be initiated.' Little Rayner hadn't been in the cubs long. His uniform was still brand new. At the side of his new uniform even Garno looked dead scruffy. We had sand and mud all over us. I was jealous of Little Rayner's brand-new green garter taps, but glad my leather woggle was old and worn and not all shiny like his, and that my neckerchief was faded.

'Akela says them other three kids can come if they want,' said Little Rayner. He nodded towards Spenco, Peggo and young Gin'er, who was standing watching us, sucking his thumb.

'They can't,' I said. 'They're catholics.'

We walked off with Little Rayner. The three kids started getting back on the fire engine. Uncle Mad didn't seem to notice that we were going.

Akela and the cubs were sitting in a circle down at the side of the lake. He didn't half look mad, and after prayers—*Teach us good Lord to serve thee as thou deservest, to give and not to count the cost, to fight and not to heed the wound*—he starts on us.

'Didn't you cubs know this was initiation night?' he bawled out when we got up to him.

'No, Akela.' *Course* we knew, but I wasn't going to tell *him* that.

'Then you should have known. And how do you think your mothers are going to get those uniforms clean?'

'Haven't got a mother,' I said. He didn't hear me. He started on Raymond Garnett. 'As for you, Raymond, I'm surprised at you. You're a sixer, you should know better.' I was hoping I would be made a sixer soon, but I bet I wouldn't be now.

Akela went chuntering on. He didn't usually speak to us in that way, like a teacher. We stood awkwardly in the middle of the circle, letting Baloo dust us down.

'If you don't want to come to cub meetings you've you've only got to say so!' snapped Akela. 'Sit down!'

We sat cross-legged in the circle, feeling silly.

'If nobody wants a cub pack I wish they'd just let me know,' chuntered Akela. 'It's all the same to me. *I* can always find plenty to do.'

He went on a bit more, then the initiation of Little Rayner began.

'*Do you know the Law and Promise of the Wolf Cub Pack?*'

'Yes, Akela, I do.'

'*What is the Law?*'

'The cub gives in to the Old Wolf. The cub does not give in to himself.'

8

WE went back to the cub hut for Taps, then I went back home. I was just taking my cub jersey off so that my Auntie Betty wouldn't see the clay on it when Marion Longbottom comes knocking on our back door to see if I would go over to Fawcett's for a minute.

I knew what *that* was in aid of before she even opened her mouth, it was to find out what had been going on with Big Rayner and them in the den that night. Might have known that Mrs *Faw*cett would come poking her big long nose into it. She was worse than our blinking teacher.

'I can't come out,' I said. 'My Auntie Betty says I've to stop in for getting my uniform mucky.'

'Well you'd better tell her that Mrs Fawcett wants to see you, because she does,' said Marion.

I didn't want my Auntie Betty to know. I said: 'No, I'm not coming.'

Marion said: 'It's *all* right, you were with me. Come on.' She was only the same age as me, but she was like right old sometimes. She could make you do something you didn't want to, just by saying: '*Come* on' in this warm voice. We went through our garden and down the street towards Fawcett's. It was getting dark by now. Some of the others were playing round the lamp post. I wished I'd been them.

I hadn't done anything in the den that day but I was scared silly.

Mrs Fawcett was *al*ways shoving her oar in every time we'd been doing anything. Whenever something went wrong, she has to poke *her* blinking neb in. That time Mono broke that big sunflower in Mrs Theaker's garden, it was Mrs Fawcett who had us all in their house and found out who'd done it. Same as when Little Rayner pinched all the parkin on bonfire night, Mrs Fawcett found out it was him.

I didn't like her. I was frightened of her because she was the only grown-up I had ever seen whose nose ran like Barbara Monoghan's or Little Rayner's. She had a lot of dirty little babies who were always crawling about in the street with just their vest on. There was a Mr Fawcett as well but you never saw him. Sometimes when you were outside their house you could hear him shouting: '*Who's in bed with their boots on?*' and: '*Who's put rabbit bones under the pillow?*' It was a funny house.

We went in by the front door, me and Marion. That was another thing about Fawcett's. They didn't keep their front door for relations and going on holiday. *Any*body could go through their front door. You didn't have to knock. You just walked in. My Auntie Betty said it was common.

The house was dirty. They were always having to have the bug van. It smelt inside, a funny smell like too much toffee. There were bits of bread on the floor, half-opened tins of Swiss milk all over the shop and big dinner plates on top of the wireless. All the furniture looked as though it had been bought second-hand. But in the corner there was this big Monopoly game that Mr Fawcett had bought for the children at Christmas. They were right dear, these Monopolies. He wouldn't let anybody play with it in case it got broken.

Kathleen Fawcett, Barbara Monoghan, and Mono were all sitting on the sofa when we went in. Big Rayner sat in an armchair with his arms spread out over the sides. He was trying to look as though he hadn't done anything. Mrs Fawcett was crouched on a three-legged stool by the fire.

Me and Marion went in and stood by the sideboard. I didn't like to sit down at Fawcett's.

Outside I could hear the others playing. 'Salt, mus-tard, vin-e-gar, PEP-per, salt, mus-tard, vin-e-gar, PEP-per,' called the lasses who were skipping. I wanted to go out and play with them. I wished I hadn't come home from the cubs so early. I wished I hadn't been to the den that day.

Mrs Fawcett folded her arms and did this big deep sigh as if she was settling down for the night. She looked at me.

'Right, now *he's* here,' she said. 'We'll get to the bottom of it.' She turned to Mono and Big Rayner.

'What-were-you-doing-in-them-*rhubarb* fields?' she said. She must have asked them about fifty times already by the sound of it.

'*No*thing, I've *told* you!' said Mono. 'Were we, Rayno?'

'*No-o!*' said Big Rayner sulkily.

'Well what were you doing in that den, then?'

'*No*thing!'

'Oh but you were!' said Mrs Fawcett. 'I'm going to have that den taken down! You'd no business to put it up!'

('Salt, mus-tard, vin-e-gar PEP-per, salt, mus-tard,

vin-e-gar PEP-per,' went the girls outside.) I stood leaning on the sideboard, staring at a hole in the oil-cloth. They had no rugs or carpets down, only this oilcloth with red squares, all worn and stringy.

'Well we'll see what *he* knows about it,' said Mrs. Fawcett, turning to me.

'Nothing, do I, Marion?' I said. My voice was shaking already.

'Well what did they tell you they'd been doing in them rhubarb fields?' said Mrs Fawcett.

'Nothing, they just said they'd been in the tusky fields. Rhubarb fields.'

'Who with?'

'Just Big Rayner and your Kathleen and Mono and Barbara Monoghan and them.'

'Who's them?' said Mrs. Fawcett.

'Just them four,' I said, nodding towards the others on the sofa.

'Ah, but we were only pinching tusky, weren't we?' chimed in Mono. He put his chin out at me eagerly.

'I don't know,' I said miserably.

'You-ou *do* know!' said Mono. 'We were only pinching tusky. *You* know.'

I remembered the night in the den, when everything was quiet outside. I remembered how I could tell that they had all been up to something. I didn't know what to say.

'What did they say about you and Marion?' asked Mrs Fawcett.

'I don't know,' I said. My heart was thumping. Outside the girls were shouting: 'Ray-mond Garn-ett ees no goo-ood!' I was listening to them in a far-off sort of way and wondering why Raymond Garnett wasn't in here as well, and I could hardly take in what Mrs Fawcett was saying.

'Did they say anything about you and Marion going in the rhubarb fields?' said Mrs Fawcett.

'We didn't, did we, man?' put in Mono.

'*You* did!' said Marion, pointing at him. It was the first time she had spoken. '*Di*dn't he? Didn't he say we'd been in the tusky fields, us two? Because Kathleen Fawcett and Barbara Monoghan said they knew something about me, and I said what?'

'I don't know,' I said.

'We were only kidding, weren't we, Kathleen?' said Barbara Monoghan. She sounded shaky as well.

'Yer, we were,' said Kathleen.

'And what have I told you about going in them rhubarb fields?' said Mrs Fawcett to Kathleen, now that Kathleen had opened her mouth. 'What have I *told* you?'

'Nothing,' said Kathleen Fawcett.

'Didn't I tell you you hadn't to go in them rhubarb fields, either with Monoghan's lad or anybody else?' said Mrs Fawcett.

'She didn't go in with me, did you, Kathleen?' said Mono.

All of a sudden Kathleen Fawcett starts flipping well crying. Her face crinkled up like a baby's and she burst out through her sobs: 'I did! I *told* you my mother'd find out and you said she wouldn't! You said she wouldn't know!'

The sobs gurgled and guzzled out of her. 'She's crying, Mrs Fawcett,' said Barbara Monoghan.

'She'll do more than cry!' said Mrs. Fawcett. 'What did I tell you about going in them rhubarb fields?' she said again to Kathleen.

'*We-ell!*' sniffled Kathleen.

'What did I *tell* you?' Mrs Fawcett got up and started hitting Kathleen on the back. 'What-did-*I*-tell-*you*?' Kathleen tried to say something but she was too choked up to make any sense.

'You can just go to bed this minute!' said Mrs Fawcett. 'And stop that chawping, before I give you something to chawp about!'

'He said we were only going pinching *tus*ky!' sobbed Kathleen. She got up and went out through the living room door.

Mrs Fawcett didn't seem bothered. 'There'll be more than one roaring by the time I've finished!' she said. We heard Kathleen crying her way upstairs.

'She said you told her she could *go* in the tusky fields!' said Mono, putting his chin out again.

'Oh, no, she didn't!' said Mrs Fawcett.

'She did, Mrs Fawcett! Didn't she, Rayno?'

'*I* don't know,' said Big Rayner.

'She did, didn't she, man?' said Mono, turning to me.

'I don't know,' I said.

'Well she did,' said Mono.

Mrs Fawcett went back and sat on her three-legged stool. 'Where's that Rayner's lad?' she said. 'Now we'll hear *his* half of the story.'

Big Rayner put on a scowl.

'*They-ey* were daring us!' he mumbled.

'Who were daring who?' said Mrs Fawcett.

'Your Kathleen and Barbara Monoghan. They were daring me and Mono.'

'Oo, you lie!' said Barbara Monoghan. 'Don't you believe him, Mrs Fawcett. You ask your Kathleen!'

'What were they daring you?' said Mrs. Fawcett.

'*To-o* got to the tusky fields.'

'What to do?' If you ask me anything, Mrs. Fawcett was having a good time with herself.

Big Rayner didn't reply.

'What were you going to do in the rhubarb fields?' said Mrs Fawcett.

'*I* don't know!' said Big Rayner.

'Yes you do know, with your "I don't know"! What were you going to do?'

'*Nothing!*'

'I shall tell your *father*!' said Mrs Fawcett.

'You *know* what we were off to do!' said Big Rayner. Suddenly I felt hot and sweaty and miserable and sick. All the whispers I didn't understand, heard in the school lavatories and from the big lads, late at night at the top of our street, came back into my mind. I just wanted to go out of Fawcett's. The smell of toffee was becoming so that I couldn't stand it. Outside I could hear the girls shouting: '*Ray-mond Garn-ett ees a foo-ool!*'

Mrs Fawcett turned to me. 'Were you and Marion Longbottom in the rhubarb fields?'

'Oo, we *weren't*, were we?' said Marion.

I said: 'Well we went *through* them, didn't we?' I was always being honest like that. I couldn't help it.

'Yes, but only on the way to Clarkson's woods, wasn't it?' said Marion.

'Yer. You ask Raymond Garnett,' I said to Mrs Fawcett.

'I'm not asking Raymond Garnett, I'm asking you!' said Mrs Fawcett. 'I'd have thought your Auntie Betty would have learnt you more sense.'

Tears came up into my eyes because it wasn't fair. I felt the same as I did that time when one of our

84

teachers said I'd got my new jersey off the Boots for the Bairns Fund, and I hadn't all the time, my Auntie Betty bought it. Just because it was the same colour.

'Well I haven't been in the blinking tusky fields,' I said. 'Only going through them with Marion and Raymond Garnett, that's all.'

'Well you don't *go* in, none of you!' said Mrs Fawcett. 'Do you hear me? None of you!'

We all muttered: '*Yer!*' We were all glad because we knew it was nearly over.

'You keep out, all of you!' said Mrs. Fawcett. 'Now *what* have you got to do?'

'Keep out,' we all mumbled.

'Well think on!' said Mrs Fawcett.

We all got up and trooped out through the front door. The lasses outside had fixed a rope to the lamp-post and they were swinging round on it.

'Hey, will she say anything?' said Mono, as soon as we were outside on the path.

'*She-e* won't say anything,' said Big Rayner. 'I wouldn't like to be in their Kathleen's shoes, though.'

'Neither would I,' said Barbara Monoghan.

'Should've told her about you and Marion Longbottom that time, Rayno,' said Mono.

They all started tittering.

9

ALL that week I had been dreading having to go to this pantomime with Ted and his mother. Not because I didn't want to get back on pals with him, it was all the same to me whether I did or I didn't; but because I knew what it would be like when I did. We hadn't spoken to each other for over a week; it was the longest time we had ever fallen out for. I could just imagine the first awkward minutes when we got back on pals again, talking to each other in strange cracked voices and clearing our throats as though we'd never met before. I only hoped he wouldn't want to shake hands, like some kids did.

I woke up that Saturday morning feeling like you do when there is an exam on at school. All through breakfast, and all the way to the Co-op and back, I kept thinking: 'Only six more hours, and I'll be going through Ted's gate.' 'Only five more hours, and we'll be sitting in the Theatre Royal.' Only four more hours, and we'll be setting off for Church Moor Feast.' It wasn't so bad when I thought: 'Only ten more hours, and I'll be back home.'

I rehearsed to myself how I would go into their house. I would rush in, panting with excitement, going: 'Hey, there's been a accident in Royal Park Crescent! A woman's got run over by that fire engine of Uncle Mad's and they've just rung up for the ambulance!' But I knew I wouldn't all the time, really.

I thought of trying to get out of it altogether, but I knew my Auntie Betty would make me go. And even when I set off for their house at five minutes to two, with my best suit on and a bar of raisin chocolate and some mint imperials in my pocket, I was wondering if I could get away with going into the park for the day. Like we did that time when we were supposed to go to Morecambe with the cubs, only we'd spent the money so we went into town instead, and came back and *said* we'd been to Morecambe, only my Auntie Betty found out that we hadn't.

I got through Ted's gate by saying to myself: 'I'm not going to stop walking until I've gone a hundred steps,' and by that time I'd gone a hundred steps I was on their side path. I stood there for a minute to get my breath back, then I thought: 'Anyway, here goes, and went and banged on their door. It was a joke knock, pom-tiddley-eye-tie, pom POM—a sort of middle between an ordinary knock and the special code knock we used to have, three longs and a short.

Ted himself came to the door, wearing his best blue trousers. 'That's right, knock the blinking door down,' he said in a sort of strained, joking voice. I could tell straight away that he had the same feeling as me.

I went in. He sat on the settee and I sat in one of the big armchairs. We both sat well back to show that we weren't worried. Ted started whistling through his teeth. His mother was upstairs.

'It'll have blinking started if she doesn't blinking hurry up,' said Ted. He spoke in a grudging voice, but it was a grudge we were supposed to share with each other.

'Why, what——' My voice had gone dry through not being used. I started again.

'Why, what time does it start?'

'Half past two. *Tells* you in the paper,' said Ted.

We talked in this way for a few minutes while his mother came downstairs. She was wearing a light blue coat with a fur collar, and carrying a shiny black handbag. Neither of us were saying anything by this time.

'What's up with you two, swallowed your tongues?' said Ted's mother.

'No, just thinking,' said Ted. He wrinkled his forehead and started clicking his fingers as though he was trying to think of something.

'Think of a number,' he said to me, trying to sound ordinary.

'Four,' I said. I cleared my throat before I spoke, this time.

'No, you haven't to tell me it. Think of a number.'

'Thought of one,' I said.

'Double it.'

'Yer.'

'Multiply by six.'

'Yer.'

'Divide by four.'

'Yer.'

'Add three.'

'Yer.'

'Take away the number you first thought of.'

'Yer.'

'Answer's seven,' said Ted.

It wasn't seven at all, it was twenty-three, because he'd done it wrong, but I didn't tell *him* that. I remembered a riddle I'd learned off of Mr Longbottom.

'What letter is like an island?' I said.

'Letter O,' said Ted.

'No, T, because it's always in the middle of water,' I said. I was breathing better now, and I could talk properly without having to gather spit in my mouth first.

'What goes up but can't come down, then?' said Ted.

'Smoke,' I said.

'Yar, you knew it,' he said. If we'd been on pals properly he would have said: 'Yar, well it isn't then, cleverclogs, it's an umbrella,' or something, but he was trying to be friends.

Ted's mother was pulling on a pair of gloves that she'd got out of the sideboard drawer.

'Come on, nattercans,' she said. She seemed in a good mood. We went out and she put the door key under the dustbin.

'Don't tell anybody where we put our key,' said Ted. It was a secret between us. We set off up our street towards the tram stop. Going past our house I looked to see if my Auntie Betty was waving, but she wasn't.

On the tram we sat in the front seats, playing at drivers. We started talking arjy parjy.

'Warjee arjee garjoing tajo sarjee Carjinderella,' said Ted.

'No, this is it,' I said. 'Warjee arjee garjoing tarjee sarjee Carjinderarjella.'

The tram passed some houses where we had once got raced by a bulldog. It reminded both of us at once.

'Where we got raced by that bulldog,' said Ted.

'Oo, yer,' I said. 'Where we pinched all them apples.' I lowered my voice so that Ted's mother couldn't hear. Whispering together on the front of the tram it was as though we had never even fallen out.

'Where we got chucked out of the Tivoli that time,' said Ted.

'Where we shouted out at that woman.'

'Where we broke old ma Theaker's gate.'

I was going to say: 'Where I bit you on the leg that time,' but I stopped myself, knowing that it wasn't time yet to laugh our quarrel off as a joke. We got off the tram and walked up to the Theatre Royal. By this time we were acting daft as though nothing had ever happened, walking with one foot in the gutter and then pulling our hands up inside our coat sleeves as though we had no arms, and making snorting noises at each other. Ted's mother just said: 'Tuh, silly half hour again.'

Can't say I thought much of the pantomime. The blinking theatre was half empty, for a start. We had the best seats in the house, right up in the gallery, but you're supposed to go see pantomimes at Christmas, not in the middle of June or whenever it was. The programme was all worn-out and creased instead of shiny, and they didn't even have the flipping neon-lights on outside.

Still, it didn't worry us. We were back on pals again and I didn't have to pretend to myself that Ted was my cousin any longer, and I had to talk to him for just five minutes, then he would be going. We sat back and laughed at everything we saw, louder than we would have laughed in the ordinary way.

Anyway, I don't know whether you know this pantomime, this Cinderella, but it's where Buttons— that's the one who runs this music shop—is trying to sell these violins to the Three Blockheads. They do all sorts. To start with, the little fat one gets his head fast in a big trumpet thing, then Buttons tries to pull him out and gets his backside stuck in a drum. Then the *other* one comes on, the one with the glasses. Oh, no, before that; this little fat one tries to pull Buttons up out of this drum, so of course, *he* falls into it himself and smashes it to bits. Then this one with the glasses starts. He gets this harp round his neck and tries to walk out through this door. Of course, the harp catches against the whatdoyoucallits, the door posts, and knocks him flying.

It was dead funny, but by this time me and Ted weren't laughing much any more. I suppose the strain of laughing all through the pantomime, even through the love songs, was beginning to show. And anyway Ted's mother had started saying: 'All right, that'll do!' Blinking misery. She had a *face* like the back of a bus smash.

Anyway, all this time the tall thin one is off the stage. Well Buttons and these other two out of the Three Blockheads, the little fat one and the one with the glasses, well they do all sorts. They finish up all piled up on the floor with violins, trumpets, triangles and all sorts on top of them. Then this tall thin one comes on, and do you know what he's riding? He's riding a bicycle.

That started it, because straight away both Ted and me were reminded of the first time we saw Uncle Mad, that time he came careering down our street on the day we had our quarrel. Ted snorted down his nose—he always used to laugh like that—and gave me a nudge that knocked my bag of mint imperials all over the floor.

'Hey, that feller!' he shouted.

Whatever had been wrong between us and Ted was now all over, and I felt a wave of gladness coming over me. My mint imperials were all over the floor. I said: 'Ah, look what you're doing, man! *Pick* 'em up!' but I wasn't bothered. I wasn't bothered about anything.

'No, look! That feller! Grr-*quack!*'

'No, this is it,' I said. 'He does *this* now. Cuit cuit cuit cuit cuit!' We both started laughing all over the place.

'Cuit cuit cuit cuit cuit! *You* do it!'

'Grrrr-*qua*-ack! Cuit cuit cuit!'

'No. Grrr-qua-ack-QUACK-*QUA-ACK!*'

It didn't matter how much row we made just then because the tall thin one was trying to ride his bike over the three fellows on the floor, Buttons and the other two, and everybody in the theatre was screaming with laughter. Ted's mother said: 'That'll do!' but she didn't stop us. I started making gargling noises. A women behind went: 'Tt!' but Ted's mother didn't hear her.

After a bit Buttons and the Three Blockheads all get up, then Prince Charming comes on. Cinderella has lost this shoe and this other lady, Prince Charming, well she's got it and she's trying to find out who it belongs to. Anyway, she starts singing this song. It is one of those blinking love songs and the Three Blockheads all stand round trying not to look funny for a change. Everybody in the audience shuts up, and right in the middle of the song Teds starts spurting out laughingly again and goes: 'Grr-*quack!*' very quietly.

I whispered: 'That feller,' and put my leg out into the aisle like we had seen Uncle Mad do when he turned the corner into Royal Park Crescent that time. Ted said: 'No, watch,' and started pulling his funny face. Every time he did his funny face he used to make his eyes go all squint-eyed, loll his tongue out, stick one shoulder up in the air and flap his hands about in front of him. His mother always used to go barmy. She saw him doing it and slapped him on the knee, going: 'Have I to tell you?' Ted turned on me and shouted: 'Sto-o-o-op it, man!' He was always doing that. The woman behind us went: 'Ssssh!' We quietened down for a bit, then a bit later on Ted started making clicking noises with his tongue and holding his breath and that. Then the Three Blockheads suddenly reminded us of the Three Stooges so we started imitating *them*, going: 'Naff naff naff naff naff' all the time.

Ted's mother leaned forward and whispered: 'If I have to tell *you* once more! Now sit up straight and give over!' She started shaking Ted up and down to make him sit up straight. I sat there keeping out of it, but suddenly remembered the Three Blockheads again and started laughing, so she tells *me* to shut up as well. Ted snorted again. I started making a funny face of my own, shoving my lower lip up as far as my nose and making spurting noises. Then I started lolloping my arms up and down like a chimpanzee. I saw the pile of mint imperials on the floor where Ted had spilled them, and started grinding them into the floor with my feet, waving my arms out and making these spurting noises as though I had gone mad.

All of a sudden this blinking usherette comes up and leans over me to speak to Ted's mother.

'If you can't keep these lads quiet I'll have to ask you to leave,' she said. 'I'm sorry, but there's other people besides you.'

Ted's mother didn't reply. She looked murder at us, then she pursed her lips together and looked straight in front of her. It was where Cinderella is trying on this slipper made out of glass.

'You've done it now, man!' whispered Ted. We looked at each other, and he suddenly went cross-eyed at me. I spurted out laughing. I couldn't help it, and once I started I couldn't stop. The woman behind went: 'They want a good hiding, pair of them!' Ted's mother got up.

'Out!' she said. She bundled Ted up and shoved him out into the aisle, me with him. She walked quickly to the red sign where it said: 'Exit.' We followed after her, going: 'What's up? What have *we* done?' to each other.

On the stairs, Ted's mother said: 'I'll give you what have we done when I get you home! You come out with me no more!' She didn't speak another word all the way home. She wouldn't let us sit next to each other, on the tram. She shoved Ted into a seat and sat next to him.

As soon as we got off the tram and into our street she starts clouting Ted over the head with her handbag. 'Get down that street,' she shouted. She seemed to have gone mad. Mono and Big Rayner were in our street, fixing skates on. They grinned at each other.

Ted covered his head up with his hands and went: 'Gi-ive up! It wasn't me, it was him!' She just went

on hitting him down the street. Big Rayner shouted:
'Belt him one, missis!'

I thought I might as well slope off, so I started
hanging back. Ted, ducking from his mother, shouted
back at me: 'It's your blinking fault! You wait!'

I didn't say anything. Ted's mother went on hitting
him and going: 'Get in that house!' Ted went: 'I-I-I'm
going to Church Moor blinking Feast!'

'You're going nowhere!' she screamed. 'I'll show
you not to make a fool out of me! With your cheek and
impudence! Get in that house!'

They were outside Ted's gate by now and she was
pushing him in. He turned round to me for the last
time. He was crying by now. He shouted: 'And don't
think I've forgotten about you biting me that time
either!' His mother shoved him in.

I set off for Church Moor Feast by myself. It was
no use waiting for Ted coming out again. And even if
he did come out again this was a quarrel that, I could
guess, would never be made up.

10

EVERY summer they used to have this big Feast on Church Moor, down past Wharfedale Avenue. Turn right near Holy Cross church and it was down there.

We had about three feasts a year, but this was the biggest of the lot. They had everything you could think of—steam swings, roller coaster, dodgems, ghost train, caterpillar. Everything. It was smashing.

Sometimes the Feast was so big it used to boil over on to the other side of the road, near the allotments.

I liked it down that way. It was the only part of our estate that was anything like. Church Moor, well it wasn't really a moor, it was just a big cinder track. When it was windy the dust used to blow up in big clouds and we used to put goggles on and ride bikes through it, like a sandstorm. On hot Sundays we would trudge through it until there was a film of dust on the toecaps of our best shoes and we could draw faces on it with our fingers.

It was best when there was a feast on, though, all bright and noisy with big cables half buried in the cinders, leading from the moon rocket and the Wall of Death, and ending up in big vans whose motors hummed in the dark corners of the moor.

Me and Ted had gone with his mother as long as I can remember, always after the pantomime. We always used to have our tea at their house, getting right excited and flicking jelly at each other, then go out to the Feast. Sometimes my Auntie Betty would come down as well and meet us there.

I walked down Coronation Grove, leaving Ted getting hit by his mother. I didn't have to have *him* with me. I could go on my own. Don't need *Ted* to go to the Feast with.

I only had threepence, but I thought I could get some more at the Feast. They had these roll-em-down stalls, where you roll a penny down and it falls on these squares. I always used to win on them. Some of the stalls had like mesh all round them and instead of just squares marked 4d, 3d, 2d, there were ten shilling notes all taped down, with sixpences on them. You had to get your penny over the sixpence to win the ten shilling note. I never won at that, though.

Sometimes I would win as much as ninepence on the stalls and then blinking lose it all again. Then I would hang around the Feast, hoping that my Auntie Betty might come and give me some money. She was always trying to win a dinner service at that stall where you get tickets and a light flashes on all these different names and if it finishes up on the name that's on your ticket, well you win. I used to wait round that stall looking for my Auntie Betty.

I walked down Coronation Grove, along Royal Park Crescent and into Carnegie Road. At the bottom of Carnegie Road I could hear the first sounds of the Feast, the steam swings and the music from half a dozen roundabouts all mixed up so that it sounded like the air raid siren they were always trying out near our school. I began to forget about Ted and sniffed for the cinder-dust smell of the Feast. I turned the corner of Carnegie Road and walked, happy, into the back-wash of the Feast, the candy-floss sticks and bits of coconut shell and brandy-snap bags that had been stamped into the street by all the people coming home. I felt sorry for them as I passed them because they had been and I was just going. Some of them carried prizes, coconuts, teddy bears, lemon squeezers, and one woman had an eiderdown. I thought it would be nice if I could win an eiderdown for my Auntie Betty, and I thought up this dream where I always won something every time I went to the Feast, and always brought home silver tea sets, eiderdowns ('Oo, you haven't brought any more eiderdowns, have you?' said my Auntie Betty), baskets of groceries from Chicken Jim's, until the stall-owners knew me and pretended to be frightened when I went near their stalls.

I walked down the cinder slope on to Church Moor, stepping over the outcrop of cables and trailer hooks round the caravans. The moor always looked different when the Feast was on, and when it was gone it looked different again, like that oily patch of concrete near the slag heaps, where they used to have Uncle Mad's fire engine.

I *saw* Uncle Mad as I turned into the first avenue of roll-em-down stalls. He was riding his bicycle through the Feast, riding slowly so that the wheels swivelled and he nearly fell off. Didn't see *me*, though.

I saw Raymond Garnett as well. He was eating potato crisps. He was the only kid in our school who could flipping well af*ford* to eat potato crisps.

He said: 'Hiya, man! Where's your mate?'

I said: 'Who? *I* don't know!' I was hoping Ted would

come down to the Feast after all, and that I would walk straight past him with a big eiderdown under my arm. 'Give us a crisp,' I said.

'*I-I* haven't had any tea, man!' said Raymond Garnett. He turned away without giving me a crisp. Near the rifles he threw the bag away and stood on it. It was still half full.

He was *like* that.

I watched him go and began to breathe in the noises and the yellow-bright lights of the Feast. A voice on a record croaked with dust went: 'The music goes round and *round*, and it comes out here.'

There was a stall called Bingo: large prizes. All the people were putting little counters on little coloured squares, and a man was shouting in language I didn't understand: 'Clickety-click, sixty-six, key of the door, twenty one. Legs eleven. Sixty-five, old age pension, Kelly's eye, number one. . .'

At one of the stalls I stopped and got one of my pennies out. I started looking at the wooden chutes where you roll your money down. Some of them were curved at the end and some of them straight. The straight ones were best. I rolled my penny down and it went on a line. A fat woman in a white overall scooped it up.

I told myself: 'I'll just have one more go and then if I don't win anything I'll go on another stall.'

I rolled a penny down again. It circled over the stall and came nearly all the way back to me. Then it fell just inside a twopence square in the last line. The fat woman had her back to me, serving someone at the other side of the stall. She turned round and saw my penny in the twopence square.

'You *put* that there!' she said.

'I didn't!' I cried. 'Did I, missus?'

'I don't know, love, I wasn't watching,' said the woman beside me. She had a new basket with a dinner plate and a Mickey Mouse in.

The fat woman flung two pennies across the stall and said: 'You don't come here again!'

I went away biting my lip to stop from crying.

I walked right through the next avenue of stalls, past the moon rocket and the bumper cars, before I had another go on another roll-em-down stall. I thought the fat woman had someone following me. I found one of those stalls with the mesh in front where you roll the pennies on to rich black cloth and try to win ten shillings.

First go my penny covered a sixpence. The man— it was a man this time—threw me three pennies and it turned out it wasn't a sixpence, just a threepenny bit. One of the pennies landed just on his side of the mesh when he threw them, and I had to scrabble under the wire with my fingers to get at it.

I had fivepence now. I held the pennies tight until they were hot in my hand. I put my hand to my face and it smelled of copper. I was going to lick it and then I remembered Marion telling me that if you do, you get cancer. I looked through the noise to see if Ted was near but I couldn't see him.

Behind me was the helter-skelter, like a lighthouse. I had never been on the helter-skelter because it cost sixpence; it was always something unreal and far away. In *Film Fun*, Laurel and Hardy always went down the helter-skelter when they got £50 given for catching a burglar, but none of the kids *I* knew went down it.

I went back to one of the stalls and rolled a penny down the chute and it was fourpence straight off, so then I had eightpence. I went up to the helter-skelter and looked at it for a bit, then I walked on again knowing all the time that I was *go*ing to have a go on it, and then I walked back. I went up to the pay box. It was like a picture house pay box with a big notice, shaped like a shield, that said in red: '1/- Children half price 1/-' Some other notices said: 'Oh U Kid!' and 'O.K. Let's Go.' I gave the girl sixpence and a man gave me like a doormat. I climbed the stairs inside the helter-skelter. It was all wooden bars and bare canvas. No one else was having a go. I stood at the top of the slide and looked out over the Feast.

I looked over the patched canvas roofs, and the strings of coloured light bulbs, waiting for someone I knew so that I could wave to them and maybe dive down the slide head first.

There was no one. I sat on the mat at the top of the helter-skelter and gripped both sides with my hands. Then below me, just at the paybox, I saw Uncle Mad with Raymond Garnett.

Uncle Mad was leaning back on his bicycle. He looked as though he was paying for a go on the helter-skelter. Raymond Garnett was standing with him.

I shouted: 'Garno! Garno! Wa-atch!' and let go. The helter-skelter wasn't much really; not much better than the slide down in the park. All the way down I was thinking: 'That's blinking sixpence gone west.'

I slid to the bottom, sprung up on my feet as though I was used to it and went over to Raymond Garnett.

'Caw, it's smashing, man! Are you going on?'

'Course I am,' said Raymond Garnett. Uncle Mad turned round and gave him the blue ticket that he had just bought at the pay box. Raymond Garnett took it without saying thank you and went up the helter-skelter with the mat.

I said: 'Caw, is he paying for you?' but he didn't hear. Uncle Mad did not seem to know that I was there.

I watched for Raymond Garnett coming down. He was frightened to come down properly. He slid down slowly, gripping hold of the sides with his hands and letting himself come down inch by inch.

I shouted up: '*Le-et* go, man!' He let go and slid to the bottom.

Uncle Mad wheeled his bicycle away and Raymond Garnett, dusting the seat of his trousers down, followed after him without speaking to me.

I went over to one of the stalls and lost my last two pennies. They were on a line. I put my hands in my pockets and began to look for money on the floor, but all I could see were the thick cables, half-buried, leading from one stall to another.

The man on the Bingo stall shouted: 'Doctor's orders num-ber nine, half a ton num-ber ten. Sweet sixteen, never been kissed. . .' I couldn't see him but I could hear him.

I wished I hadn't gone on the blinking rotten helter-skelter and I began to feel miserable.

There was cinder dust in my eyes and in my ears and up my nose and I could even feel it gritting in my hair. I started pulling bits out of my hair and stood there doing it until some kids walked past and one of them said: 'Want to get the nits out of your swede, kid.'

I started walking on a length of cable, seeing if I could walk it without falling off, and it led me up to the Speedway.

I shoved my way through the crowd to where Raymond Garnett was, standing on the steps, watching the motor bikes whirr round. I *knew* he'd be there. Uncle Mad wasn't with him, though.

I said: 'Hey, Garno, did Uncle Mad pay for you on that thing?'

'Course he did,' said Garno.

'What did he pay for you for?'

'*I* don't know,' said Garno. 'Cos he wanted to. He's off to pay for me on the Speedway as well.'

'Ha! Bet he is! Where is he, then?'

'Just gone home to take his bike in. Then he's coming back.'

I said: 'Bet he is!' I asked Raymond Garnett to lend me a penny only he wouldn't. He said he was stoney broke and turned his pockets inside out to prove it.

'Well let's have a look in your *coat* pocket, then!' I said, but he wouldn't. I *knew* he was lying. He was *always* lying.

I stood for a minute, watching the motor bikes going round and hearing the music that sounded as if it were being strained through wire wool. Then the go ended and people started rushing to get the best bikes.

I walked away, to the stall where they have these tickets, hoping to see my Auntie Betty, but she wasn't there. I watched the light flickering from one name to another—Ann—David—John—Betty—and pretended I had got a ticket with David on it. But the light stopped at Eunice, and a woman who had Eunice on her pink ticket won this big Whistling Boy. I stood with my hands in my pockets and my lips puckered, hoping she'd think I was the model for the Whistling Boy, but she didn't notice.

I was getting even more miserable. I began to feel sorry for the three or four stalls that were closed down, covered in tarpaulins. I went over and touched one of them to make it feel it had a friend, then I thought this would be unfair on the others so I started at one end of the Feast and worked my way back to the other end, touching every stall on my way and smiling at it.

It was getting late. Near the ghost train I saw Raymond Garnett for the *fourth* time, and this time Uncle Mad *was* with him. I couldn't tell it was Uncle Mad at first, because he had changed his clothes when he went to take his bike in. He was wearing like a dark blue suit, wearing it very importantly like you wear a Sunday suit, although his one was scruffier than a Sunday suit. This was the first time I'd seen him in anything different from his old blazer and flannels.

They looked as though they were going out of the Feast. I didn't know which way they were going because you can never tell which way you are in the middle of a feast, but I could tell they were *going* out.

Raymond Garnett was holding Uncle Mad's hand. He didn't look as though he wanted his hand holding and I could tell just by looking at the back of his head that he was feeling hot and silly like you do when an old woman starts kissing you.

I watched them going and soon they were out of sight past the pea-and-pie barrow and the high balloons on the edge of the Feast.

A woman's voice behind me said: '*Never* mind, love! Here, take this home for your mother!'

'Haven't got a mother,' I said. I looked round and it was the woman who had been next to me on that stall where that fat woman said I'd put it there myself and I hadn't all the time. She still had her new basket with the Mickey Mouse in it, but the white dinner plate she held in her hand, and she was giving it to me.

'I said: 'Kyou!' in a strangled sort of way and took the plate. It had all dust and straw on it. I wiped it clean with my sleeve and started to leave the Feast.

The side I went out of led up Wharfedale Avenue. Just in front of me I could see Uncle Mad and Raymond Garnett. They were still walking together but they weren't holding hands any more.

I set off home with my dinner plate, to tell my Auntie Betty I'd won it.

11

GET back into our street, and the first person I see is Ted, standing with Mono and Big Rayner outside their gate. I didn't think his mother would have let him out to play. Anyway, didn't bother me whether he was out or in. I started to walk straight past without saying anything, just like I had thought of myself doing so many times. The three of them were stuck at the gate, watching me go past. Mono still had his skates on, but Big Rayner, he had taken his off. Ted was sitting on their gate. The other two were leaning up against it.

My legs felt shaky under me as I got up to them. I didn't know whether to say anything to Mono and Big Rayner or not, because I hadn't fallen out with *them*, only with Ted. I thought I wouldn't say anything, I would just wag my head at Mono, and that would be enough. I did that; I wagged my head. The three of them just stared at me. Then Mono started mocking me, wagging *his* head about as though he had just had a fit, and I knew that Ted had got them on to his side.

I got past them and walked on up Coronation Grove. I thought: that's that, then. Big Rayner shouts up the street: 'Give us your dinner plate, tich!' but I thought he was only playing. I turned round and called out: 'No fear!' I walked a few steps backwards to show that I wanted to be friends. Then Big Rayner goes:

'Wrap it round your ear if you talk like that to me!'
Mono went: 'Don't we want hold of him, Rayno?'
Ted says nothing. Big Rayner takes a piece of paper
out of his pocket and pretends to read my name on it.
He said: 'Yer, we do!' and pretended to make a tick
on this piece of paper. Then suddenly he shouted: 'And
we're going to get him as well!' He leaped forward
and started running after me. I turned round and
pelted across the street and up Coronation Grove. Big
Rayner came after me, running as he always did,
swinging his arms from side to side like a pendulum
on one of these big clocks that they have, and lolloping
along with big strides. Mono came charging behind
him on his roller skates. Ted stayed where he was, sitting
on their gate. It was either him or Mono who shouted:
'Watch out, Rayno, he bites!' I wasn't sure which it
was.

Big Rayner was *al*ways wanting hold of people.
Just because he was bigger than they were. He thought
he was tough. He was always writing *eff-you-see* on
people's walls. It was him that took Raymond Garnett's
bike off him that time. I didn't know what he wanted
hold of *me* for, but I wasn't waiting to see.

I pelted up the street. I had got the programme
from Cinderella rolled up down my stocking and it was
catching against my kneebone as I ran. The dinner
plate that the woman at the Feast had given me, I
tried to push it under my jersey but it slipped and broke
on the ground. Mono shouted: 'Hah, blinking butter-
fingers has dropped his plate!' I didn't look round. My
shoes were becoming unfastened and my trousers were
working down at the back under my belt. I was
uncomfortable. I couldn't let Big Rayner catch me. He

used to punch people on top of your head. It doesn't hurt much but it makes you want to cry.

I thought I could run into Mono's garden near the top of our street. I got in through the gate then I saw Mono coming galloping after me on his skates. They were not strapped to his feet properly and he was running on the tips of his toes like a blinking dancer. He shouted: '*Out* of our garden!' I scrambled over the wires into the next garden and ran up the street into Parkside, towards our school.

Big Rayner was only about two lamp posts behind. My handkerchief was coming out through a hole in my pocket and I could feel it on my leg. I crossed the road like we did when we were daring one another, clearing it in seven right big strides. I lost my handkerchief in the middle of the road. 'Hah, he's lost his snot-rag now!' shouted Mono.

Big Rayner pelted over the road after me. He called out: 'You get him the other way.' Mono skated off down the far side of the road, the side I had just left. *He* was all right, it was downhill. I was running at the nose and I had this aching pain behind my teeth and my chest was sweating.

I got as far as our school gates. I touched hold of the iron railings and then I felt this big weight as Big Rayner jumped on my back. I sprawled down on the ground, catching my knee on the gravel.

'Now then,' said Big Rayner. 'I want hold of you, don't I?'

I stood up and pulled my stocking over my knee. It was bleeding and pocked with grit. I saw Mono skating up from the other side of the road.

'*Don't* I?'

108

Big Rayner sniffled and breathed heavily through his mouth. I wanted to do the same, only I daren't. Big Rayner took this piece of paper out of his pocket and pretended to read my name on it again. It was a piece of graph-paper that he must have got out of the metalwork class.

'Let's see what I want hold of you for,' he said. He held the paper right up to his nose and started moving his head from side to side as if he was reading something.

'Biting that kid's leg,' said Mono.

'Oo, yer,' said Big Rayner. 'Who said you could bite that kid's leg?' he said.

'What kid?' I said, snuffling. 'Don't know what you're on about.'

'*You* know what kid,' said Big Rayner. 'That mate of yours. Ted. Who said you could bite his leg?'

He didn't care whose leg I bit, it was just so he had some excuse for wanting hold of me.

I said: 'He bit me first.'

'Only monkeys bite,' said Mono.

Big Rayner started into me with his shoulder.

'Cock or hen?' he said.

'Chicken,' I said.

That was supposed to be the *funny* reply. If you said cock, you had to fight. If you said hen, it meant you were yellow.

'Cock or hen?' said Big Rayner.

I straddled my arms along the railings, trying to look as though I didn't care, and I said: 'I'm not frightened of *you*.'

Mono shouted: '*Slosh* him, man!'

'Cock or hen?'

I couldn't say chicken again, so I didn't say anything. Mono shouted: 'He goes out with lasses.'

Big Rayner put up his fists. 'Cock or hen?'

'Cock or *hen*?' he said again.

'Hen.'

'You're yellow, aren't you?'

I said again: 'I'm not frightened of *you*.'

'Cock or hen, then?'

'Hen.'

There was rust on my hands from the railings, and I could smell the hot gravel on the road. Mono had got my handkerchief and was running his skates over it.

'Cock or hen?'

Up the road I could see Mrs. Longbottom coming towards us, carrying some stuff in a bucket, and my heart jumped. She must have been collecting some things from their old house where they used to live.

I said to Big Rayner: 'Yur, you think you're somebody, don't you?'

'*Shur*-rup, specky four-eyes,' said Big Rayner.

'Yer, just cos I used to wear glasses,' I said.

Mono seemed to know Mrs Longbottom. He shouted out: 'Where do you get them elephants from, missus?' She was carrying like a big gold elephant under one arm, and this bucket in the other. She didn't reply, or if she did, I never heard her. 'Did you get it out of the Feast?' shouted Mono.

'Who said you could bite that kid's leg?' said Big Rayner.

I didn't take any notice of him any more. I shouted: 'Mrs Longbottom, do you want any errands running?'

Big Rayner went: 'Pipe down, man! *She* won't say anything!'

I called out: 'He's hitting us!'

Big Rayner said: '*She* won't touch us!'

I said: 'Why won't she?'

'Cos she won't,' said Big Rayner. 'She knows me, don't you, Mrs Longbottom?'

Mrs Longbottom was right up to us. I saw that she was short of breath and that she could hardly carry this bucket and this elephant. She didn't say anything, she just put her lips together and stared straight ahead, like Ted's mother at the pantomime.

'Have I to carry your elephant?' I said.

'*She* won't touch us, she's too fat,' said Big Rayner. Mrs Longbottom walked on. Mono followed her on his skates and started pulling faces behind her back. I could hear him singing out: 'Rule Britannia, two tanners make a bob, three make eighteenpence and four two bob.' He got that off Little Rayner.

'Wonder where she used to live, that woman?' I said to Big Rayner, even though I knew she used to live in Parkside. I was hoping he didn't want hold of me any more.

'Up-a-knock-a-down-street, three doors up.' said Big Rayner.

'No, where did she live?'

'In a bottle under the sink,' said Big Rayner.

Mono and Mrs Longbottom had gone round the corner into our street. She hadn't even spoken once. I bet she was going straight to our house to tell my Auntie Betty it was me.

'Who said you could bite that kid's leg?' said Big Rayner.

I said: '*We-e* were only playing.'

'Who said you could bite it?'

'I didn't *bite* it!'

'Who said you could bite it?'

'*Nobody!*'

'Cock or hen, then?' said Big Rayner.

'Hen.'

'Cock or hen?'

'Hen.'

'Cock or hen?'

'Hen.'

12

Don't ask me why, but there was blue murder at school next Monday morning over Raymond Garnett letting Uncle Mad pay for him at the Feast.

Who found out I *don't* know, but somebody must have seen him and told one of the teachers. It wasn't me, I know that much.

Anyway, just before we were going into the hall for gym Old Webby—he was our teacher—asked everyone who had been to the Feast that Saturday night to put their hands up.

I put up my hand, along with four or five others, and Raymond Garnett put *his* hand up as well. Thought he wasn't going to at first.

Old Webby said: 'Yes, Garnett, we know *you* were there. You boys don't come into gym. You go into Mr Pyecroft's class and wait there.'

We put our hands down and all the other kids started muttering: 'Oo, lucky you! Dead jammy!' One or two more kids put their hands up and said *they'd* been to the Feast, only Old Webby didn't believe them.

The class trooped out down to the gym, then me and Raymond Garnett and these other kids that had been to the Feast went down to the corridor to old Piedish's room. It was good to be roaming round the school at this hour, tripping each other up on the wooden-block floor and jumping up outside classroom doors to see who was in them, but we all wondered what was wrong.

'Bet we've got to write a composition about the Feast for that book,' said one of the kids. For months Old Croggy, the head teacher, had been trying to get us all to write this school magazine. It was going to be called The Templar after some knights who used to live near our school in the olden days. Old Croggy kept asking for boys who'd been to the pictures the week before, then he would put them all in an empty classroom and make them write compositions about it. They were never any good. I never wrote anything, because I had a school magazine of my own called the Parkside Gazette.

We came to old Piedish's door with the green curtain hanging over the glass. Old Piedish was in charge of 3C. He was all right. 3C was the noisiest class in the school and he used to be pals with all the kids in the class, pretending that they would all be hung when they left school. He used to get dead sarky and say things like: 'Perhaps Mr Rayner over there would rather be outside,' when Little Rayner was looking out of the window. Little Rayner would say: 'Yes, sir!' He was dead cheeky. Then Old Piedish would say: 'When you're in prison, Rayner, you'll be able to hang on to the bars and look out.'

Once in a blue moon he would get mad and yank a boy out of his desk by the hair and run him up the aisle to the front of the class. He was all right, though. *We* used to have him when we were in 2A.

We all trooped into Old Piedish's classroom. There

were some more kids there, some from 3B, some from 3C, and some from some of the other classes. The rest of 3C were in gym with 3A.

'Ah, another tribe!' said Old Piedish. He told us to sit down and we sat at these yellow polished desks that looked funny at the side of ours. Ours were brown. We started waving to kids we knew and hissing for kids to come and sit next to us.

'All right, simmer down!' said Old Piedish. We started looking in the desks and reading other people's exercise books. I was sitting at a kid called Jackie Warner's desk. I started going through his belongings. I opened his arithmetic book and read his name on the front. Inside the cover he had written: 'If this book should chance to roam, smack its bum and send it home.' 'Bum' was crossed out and inked in so the teacher could not tell what he had written. I looked through his sums and they were all marked three out of ten and four out of ten in red. I always got nine out of ten.

'Which one of you specimens is Mr Garnett?' says Old Piedish, looking at a register. Garnett put up his hand. Piedish didn't know him. Garnett had never been in his class.

'Yes, well the head teacher wants to see you. Off you go!'

Garnett slid out of his desk and walked to the door. He looked a bit white.

'Hurry yourself up, lad!' called Old Piedish. 'He's not going to eat you!'

Raymond Garnett went out.

'All right, settle down!' said Old Piedish. 'Now, then, let's see who we've got here. Pearson. . . Appleyard. . . Thompson. Aren't you in jail yet, Thompson?' He called out the names of some of the boys who had been in his class the year before.

'No sir,' said Thompson. He wasn't supposed to answer. Old Piedish didn't take any notice.

'We're going to do some geography while we're waiting,' he said. 'Have all you boys done Australia?'

I wondered: waiting for *what*?

Some of the kids out of 2B put their hands up. '*We* haven't, sir!'

'Then pay attention and you'll learn something the rest of 2B don't know. What boy can tell me the principal products of Australia?'

I knew them. *In Australia, wheat, maize and barley are to be had. Sheep are also to be got.* I let the other kids answer. They craned out of their desks, stretching their arms up to the ceiling and going: 'Sir! Sir!' in hoarse whispers.

'What boy can name the capitals of Australia?'

Brisbane is the capital of Queensland. Sydney is the capital of New South Wales. Perth is the capital of Western Australia. Adelaide is the capital of South Australia. I let the others shout them out.

'Brisbane, sir!'

'Brisbane, yes. Any more?'

'Sir! Perth, sir!'

'Any more?'

'Adelaide!'

'Any more?'

'Wellington!'

'Not Wellington. Wellington is the capital of—— Any boy? Wellington is the capital of——?'

New Zealand. I wondered what Old Croggy wanted Raymond Garnett for.

'Hands on heads!' went Old Piedish. Some kids were making a noise. 'Hands down! Hands on heads! Hands down! 's on heads! 's down!'

Through the French windows I could see Raymond Garnett. He had just come out of the arches where the milk crates were stacked and he was crossing the playground towards the school gate. He was going home. It was nearly an hour before dinner time.

Old Piedish saw him as well. He said: 'I don't want to hear any noise. I shall be just out in the corridor.' He went out of the room. I knew he had gone to see Old Croggy.

There was a low murmur in the classroom. People began shoving each other and whispering: '*Gi-ive up*, man!' Some kids were spitting at each other, gathering the spit on the end of one finger and flicking it with another finger. I looked round the room, at the pictures of flowers crayoned on black paper, the dark green and cream walls, the pile of dirty red history books on a table in the corner.

After a bit Old Piedish came back with Old Croggy. Old Croggy came in as he always did, walking slowly and looking at us all over his glasses as though he had caught us doing something.

'Quite still,' said Old Croggy. It was one of his sayings. He walked over to Old Piedish's desk.

Old Piedish said: 'Now pay attention. Does anyone know of anybody not here who was at the Feast on Saturday night?'

Nobody said anything. We all sat with our arms folded and looked at the other kids' backs.

'3C,' said Old Piedish. 'Is anyone from 3C missing?'

Some of the kids turned round as if they expected to see somebody come up from out of the floorboards.

'3B? Anyone from 3B?'

'No, sir,' said one of the kids.

'3A. What about 3A?'

Nobody said anything. Suddenly Old Croggy spoke. 'Come along, 3A, it's not tale-telling!'

Appleyard and Pearson, two of the kids in our class, started shoving each other. Then Appleyard puts his hand up.

'I think Patterson was there, sir!' Forgot to tell you, that was Ted's second name. First *I* knew about him going to the Feast. His mother must have let him go out straight after I'd left.

'Are you sure Patterson was there?' said Old Croggy.

'Think so, sir.'

'Did any other boy see him?'

'Yes, sir, cos he was on them swings when we passed him,' chimes in Pearson.

'Appleyard, go down to the hall and ask Mr Webb to let Patterson come here,' said Old Piedish.

Old Croggy muttered something to Old Piedish and went out. Old Piedish waited a minute and called out: 'All right—you four!' He pointed to the four kids who were sitting nearest the door, then went and sat at his desk, taking no more notice of them.

The kids all looked puzzled and whispered to each other: 'Did he say me?' Then one of them got up and said: 'What, sir?'

'Haven't you gone yet? Head teacher's room, of course!'

They went out. 'Talk quietly among yourselves,' said Old Piedish to the rest of us. '*Quietly*, I said!'

Then Appleyard comes back in with Ted. Ted was wearing just his blue gym shorts and his running shoes. He looked dead crackers, standing there shivering.

'Well,' said Old Piedish. 'You're a blockhead, aren't you?'

'Yes, sir!' said Ted. He tried to grin and started scratching the back of his leg with the lace-holes in his running shoe.

'Nothing to laugh about!' snapped Old Piedish, suddenly changing. 'Get that silly grin off your face and stand still!'

Ted stood to attention. His shorts had slipped and he was showing his belly button.

'Why didn't you come out when you were asked if you went to the Feast?'

'Don't know, sir!'

'Were you at the Feast?'

''s sir!'

'Then why didn't you come out?'

'Don't know, sir!'

'Who did you go to the Feast *with*?'

Ted nodded his head towards me. 'I was off to go with him only he bit me, sir.'

'Never mind about him for the time being. Who did you go with?'

''self, sir!'

'Get changed and come back here in five minutes!' said Old Piedish. Ted went out.

'Rest of you go on with what you were doing,' said Old Piedish. '*Quietly!*'

The four kids who had gone out did not come back again.

'You can go home when you've been in to see Old

Croggy,' whispered the kid next to me. After about twenty minutes Old Piedish looked at his wristlet watch and sent another four out.

'If the rest of you can't talk quietly we'll do some arithmetic!' he snapped. We were all getting fed up. It was nearly quarter to twelve. Out in the playground the first few were going home to their dinner, the few early ones who lived at the far side of the estate or who had some other excuse for leaving early.

'Next four!' called Old Piedish. It was me in this four. We got up and walked down the corridor. Already some of the classes were coming out, though not fast enough to be racing down the corridors as they did when the whole school came out at dinner-time.

We turned into the head-teacher's corridor. Pearson, one of the kids out of the four just before us was waiting outside the head teacher's door.

'You've to wait here,' he said.

'What's he want us for?' I whispered, but Pearson wouldn't say anything. You were not supposed to talk in the head teacher's corridor.

A kid came out of the head teacher's room and said to Pearson: 'He wants you.' He walked away trying to look as though he hadn't been caned. One of the kids called after him in a whisper: 'What's he want?' The kid stood at the end of the corridor going: 'Huh-hoo, you wait!'

Pearson came out about five minutes later, trying not to grin. He jerked his finger towards the head teacher's door to show that I was wanted next.

I knocked on the door and Old Croggy shouted: 'Come in!' I went in and walked over to his desk, trying to walk in a straight line. The room smelt of Sunday. The only thing I could see, because it blotted everything else out, was the thick yellow cane that lay on top of a cupboard. I had only once seen it used. If you were caned by the head teacher you had your name put in the black book, and if your name was put in the black book three times you were supposed to be sent to the reform school, although I never heard of that happening.

Old Croggy was sitting at his desk. He looked at me over his glasses, put the tips of his fingers together, and said: 'Yes, and what's *your* name?'

I told him my name.

'Whose class are you in?' He spoke sharply.

'Mr Webb's, sir.'

'How old are you?'

I told him how old I was. He didn't say anything for a bit. Then he said: 'Were you at the Feast last night?'

''s sir,' I said in a low voice. I cleared my throat.

'Are you sure?'

'Yes sir!'

'Did you go by yourself, or did you go with your mother?'

'By myself, sir.'

'Didn't you go with a friend, even?'

'No sir.'

'Haven't you got any friends?'

'Yes sir.'

'Well speak up—who *are* your friends?'

'Ted Patterson and them, sir.'

'Who's "them"?'

'Monoghan and Rayner and them, sir.'

'Were they at the Feast?'

'I didn't see them, sir.'

Old Croggy stopped for a minute, then speaking slowly, as though he were talking to somebody who was a bit deaf, he said: 'Did anyone give you any *mon*ey on Saturday night?'

'Only my Auntie Betty, sir.'

'How much did your auntie give you?'

'Threepence, sir, only I won another fivepence.' I told him that in case he'd seen me on the helter-skelter.

'Did anyone at the Feast give you any money?'

'No sir.'

'No one at all?'

'No sir.'

'Did anyone *offer* you any money?'

'No sir. A lady gave me a plate, sir.'

'Who else gave you something?'

'*No*body, sir!' I said in a high voice.

'Has any man ever given you any money?'

'Only once, sir.' I remembered once going off to town by myself. A man stopped me outside the Astoria and asked me to go with him because it was his birthday. He gave me a shilling and then he asked me to go a walk with him. We went for a walk as far as Christ Church. There was an air raid shelter just outside Christ Church, and he asked me to go in it with him. He said he had always wondered what it looked like inside. He asked me to go in, but I was suddenly frightened. He tried to drag me in by the sleeve. I pulled myself free and ran all the way down to the tram sheds. The shilling I always meant to put in the collection at church, but I spent it.

'A man once gave me sixpence in town, sir,' I said. I don't know why I made it sixpence. It was a shilling.

'Why did he give you sixpence? Did you know him?'

'No sir. He said it was his birthday.'

'Did you go anywhere with him?'·

'No sir.'

'Are you sure?'

'He—wanted me to go to the Astoria with him, sir, but I said I had to go home.'

'And did you go home?'

'Yes sir.'

'And what did this man do?'

'Nothing sir. He went away.'

'Did you tell your mother about this?'

'Haven't got a mother, sir.'

'Well whoever looks after you, then. Do you live with your auntie?'

'Yes sir.'

'Well tell *her*,' said Old Croggy sharply. 'And tell her I told you to. Now listen to me. If anyone ever offers you money you must say, thank you very much but I would rather not. Have you got that?'

'Yes sir.'

'Say it, then.'

'Thank you very much but I would rather not, sir.'

'And if anyone asks you to go anywhere with him, no matter where it is, tell him you've got to go home and then go straight to a policeman. Anywhere at *all*. Is that clear?'

'Yes sir.'

'Now don't forget. What have you got to do if a man asks you to go anywhere with him?'

'I've to say I've got to go home and then find a policeman, sir.'

'Do you know why?'

'No sir.'

Old Croggy suddenly started talking about something else.

'Where does your father work?'

'He's dead, sir.' I waited for him to say he was sorry, but he didn't.

'Does your auntie work?'

'No, sir.'

He looked down at a yellow HB pencil he had been fiddling with. Outside I could hear them coming out of school and banging on the dustbins in the playground.

'No one gave you any money at the Feast on Saturday night?' he said suddenly.

'No sir!'

'Did anyone pay for you a ride on anything?'

'No sir.'

'Do you know any boy from this school who *was* paid for?'

I remembered Raymond Garnett, with Uncle Mad.

'I saw one of the boys with a gentleman, sir,' I said.

'Which gentleman?'

'That gentleman that has that fire engine, sir.'

'Who did you see with him?'

'I think it was Raymond Garnett, sir.'

Old Croggy seemed to lose interest suddenly. 'All right, off you go,' he said. I was at the door when he called me back again. 'What have you got to tell your auntie?'

'About that man who gave me that money, sir,' I said.

Old Croggy followed me to the door. The other three kids were waiting in the corridor. 'You three come back this afternoon,' he said.

The playground was empty when we went out into it. We all began to run, worried in case we would be late for school in the afternoon. 'What does he want you for?' one of the kids asked me. '*No*thing,' I said.

I ran home feeling important but worried and a bit frightened. I didn't tell my Auntie Betty what Old Croggy had told me to tell her, and I started worrying in case she met him and *he* told her, or in case he asked me again if I had told her. I was late for school that afternoon. Nobody said anything. Raymond Garnett didn't turn up all afternoon.

13

NEVER got back on pals with Ted after that. He got the cane off Old Croggy for not coming out when Old Webby asked who'd been to the Feast, and he blamed me for it.

What we always did after falling out, we didn't used to speak to each other for ages, just used to walk past each other without saying anything, then after a bit we would go up and shake hands.

Only this time it was different. That playtime after we'd all been to see Old Croggy I saw Ted in the playground having a game of beddy with Mono and Little Rayner and them. He didn't take any notice of me, but he knew I was watching him, because he was trying to look as though he didn't care.

I walked off towards where some of the other kids were banging on the dustbins. I had just got up to them when Ted rushes up and jumps on my blinking back. I thought he was still playing beddy and this was his way of asking me to have a game.

'You're a ton weight, man!' I said, trying to sound as though we were still on pals. Ted didn't speak to me but raised his voice up so the others could hear. He was digging his feet into me and going: 'Gerd up, there! Gerd up!' The others started laughing and Mono shouted: 'Look at Tom Mix and his rubber donkey!' Ted was just showing off.

When we happened to be on our own together, though, he didn't speak to me at all. We sat next to each other in school, but all the time he would turn away from me and talk to kids him and me didn't like before we fell out.

One day he came up to me in the playground and holding out his hand he said: 'Shake!'

I put out my hand.

'Spear!' said Ted. He jabbed me in the stomach with the hand he had held out.

After that he started doing stupid tricks every time the others were near. We always had to line up before we went into school, and when we marched in he used to get behind me and try to tread my heels down. Once he got my shoe right off. I had to drop out to put it on again, and as I was standing on one foot Little Rayner pushes me and I fell over.

I *knew* Ted. He was trying to get all the other kids on his side. Every playtime I could see him whispering to kids and then they would come up to me and go: 'Have you gorram?' I'd have to say what, then they'd say: 'Spots on your borram.' That was one of Ted's stupid sayings. Then he used to get kids to come up and say: 'He's my pal, aren't you?' and slap me on the back so hard that it hurt.

Even Raymond Garnett used to come up and go: 'Poooh!' and hold his nose as though I'd just let off. He would have been the worst of the lot if he'd got the chance. Up till then it was always him that used to be in for it at school. Everyone used to pinch his marbles off him and snatch his cap and that. He wore this blue school cap with a badge on it. They used to shout 'College cad' at him because he was always top of the class. Bet he wasn't half glad they were picking on me for a change.

Anyway, round about this time there was one of these elections going on that they have, where they all vote. We used to go round with wads of paper tied on to a piece of string saying: 'Red or blue?' to each other. These were the different sides that they voted for, red and blue. If you were red and the person with the wad of paper was blue he would hit you with it. You nearly always got hit because he was always changing his colour.

One day Ted started on at me with one of these wads of paper.

'Red or blue?' he said.

It just so happened that I knew there was another colour in this election, and that was yellow, because somebody had told me. None of the kids knew that there was this other colour and I felt right good about it and I was dying to tell somebody.

'Red or blue?' said Ted.

'Yellow,' I said.

'Cur, did you hear that? He says he's yellow!' shouts Ted. This was in our street. All the others were there, Mono, Little Rayner and Raymond Garnett and them.

'I-I didn't say anything of the sort!' I said. 'Don't you know what yellow is?'

'Yer, you,' said Ted.

'Fancy not knowing they have yellow,' I said.

Ted looked at the others and started screwing his finger into the side of his head. 'Screwy!' he said.

'It's you that's blinking screwy, man!' I said. 'Doesn't know what yellow is.'

'What is it, man?' said Ted, grinning at the others.

'It's like red and blue. They vote for it.'

'*They-ey* don't, man! They only have red and blue!'

'Yer, well that's all *you* know, cos they have yellow as well.'

Ted didn't say anything, so I went: 'Cur, didn't even know *that*!' He still just stood there. I got braver and said: 'Not me that's blinking screwy, it's you!'

Ted looked at the others and I suddenly saw that he had just been leading me on. 'He's asking for it, isn't he?' he said.

'Yer, and he's going to get it!' chimed in Raymond Garnett.

I wasn't taking that for *one*. Not from Raymond blinking Garnett.

'What's up with *you*?' I said.

'Nothing, what's up with you?' said Raymond Garnett.

'Do you want hitting or something?' I said. I didn't want to hit Raymond Garnett or anybody else. I just thought he'd go away and they'd all leave me alone, that's all.

But instead of going away he went: 'Why, who's going to do it?'

'Me, if you're not careful,' I said. All the other kids stood round like tom moggies.

'You and whose army?' said Raymond Garnett.

That wasn't what I thought he'd say. Garno always used to be dead yellow. He was always getting bashed because he daren't stick up for himself. There was only one thing I could say now and that was: 'Do you want a fight or something?' so I said it. *That* shut him up. He wouldn't say anything.

Then blinking Mono starts pushing him into me. 'What's up?' said Mono. 'You can beat *him*, can't you?'

'Course I can,' said Raymond Garnett.

'Well why don't you, then?' said Little Rayner.

'I *will* do,' said Raymond Garnett.

'Let's *see* you then,' I said.

'That field near our school, four o'clock tomorrow,' said Raymond Garnett. That was where they always had fights. There was always a big ring of kids round to watch them, and sometimes the teachers came up on their way home and banged whoever it was that was fighting's heads together.

Little Rayner started dancing round. 'Oh, there's off to be a fi-ight!' he sang. 'Oo, you wait!' he said to me. 'He'll *bray* you, man!'

'Him and whose army?' I said. Wasn't frightened of Raymond *Gar*nett. He was tall but right thin and everyone was always hitting him so I didn't see why I couldn't as well.

They all went off, leaving me standing there under the lamp post. 'Couldn't box kippers!' I shouted. 'Take a man, not his shirt!'

'You wait till tomorrow night!' shouted Raymond Garnett.

Mono was whispering to him and showing him uppercuts or something. Little Rayner started singing, as he always did when someone was in trouble and it wasn't him. He started singing: 'All things bright and beautiful' in his cracked voice. On the other side of the road a kid out of our school stopped Ted and went: 'Red or blue?' 'Yellow, why?' went Ted. I closed my fists together and went home and sat in the hole at the top of our garden, thinking about having a fight with *Ted* and knocking him for six.

14

THE whole school knew about the fight next morning. I was a bit frightened in case any of the teachers got to know about it, but proud in a way because I was so famous. All day me and Raymond Garnett kept out of each other's way. I thought I could beat him with one hand tied behind my back, but as the day wore on I started getting like a sinking feeling and wanting to go to the lavatory all the time. I didn't want to go back to school after dinner and I wished I could break my leg. But I knew I would have to go, and on the way back to school Ted shouted after me: 'Have you made your will out?'

Anyway, that afternoon while we were having geography I was balancing my inkwell on the edge of my desk and it went and tipped up and spilt ink all over the floor. Old Ma Bates was taking us that afternoon and she was in a bad temper. She went: 'You clumsy article! Now you stay in after four o'clock and wipe it up!' I felt as though a lead weight had been lifted out of my stomach and I breathed in heavily. Next to me Ted whispered: 'Needn't think you're getting away with it, cos you're not!' But there was a chance, though. For all I knew Old Ma Bates would keep me in till half-past four.

The bell went for going-home time and Old Ma Bates said everyone could go. I thought for a minute she was going to forget about keeping me in, but she didn't. 'You get to and clean that mess!' she said. Ted whispered: 'We'll be waiting for you, so don't try to get away.'

I started mopping at the floor with bits of old blotting paper, soaking the ink in as slowly as I could. Old Ma Bates sat at her desk marking exercise books. Once I looked up and saw Ted and Little Rayner peering in through the French windows. Ted was pretending to slit his throat with his finger. Soon they went away. I finished cleaning up the ink off the floor and sat at my desk with my arms folded, hoping Old Ma Bates wouldn't look up.

It must have been about quarter-past four when she closed her exercise books and said: 'You can go now, and don't let me catch you touching those inkwells again!' I walked slowly out of the classroom, down the corridor and out of the main entrance with 'BOYS' printed up over it in stone, through the half-closed trellis gates and into the playground. At first it looked as though the others had gone but then I saw them all standing up near the railings—Ted, Little Rayner, Mono and Raymond Garnett.

'Thought he wouldn't come out!' said Little Rayner.

'Has he got his coffin with him?' said Ted.

We walked out of the playground and round by Parkside towards the fighting field. We walked without saying anything. The only one who spoke was Ted who said: 'Got any chewy?' to Little Rayner, and that was the only thing that was said.

I was frightened when we got down on to the field, not by Raymond Garnett but by this big crowd of kids who had waited to see the fight. At the same time I was happy because they were waiting to see me and Raymond Garnett and nobody else.

There was a big ring of kids round the grey patch that was worn in the grass, where the fights were always held. They parted to let us through, and looking round I saw hundreds of other kids teeming on to the field after us, some of them running. Little Rayner shoves his way to the front, singing: 'Whipsey-diddle-de-dandy-dee,' this stupid song we had to learn at school.

I had never had a fight before. I felt important and pleased at the crowds who were round us, none of them touching us but leaving it to us to have our fight.

'Back a bit,' I said, and I was right pleased when they moved back. I took off my coat and handed it to a kid I did not know. He took it and held it carefully over his arm, and this pleased me too.

Raymond Garnett took off his coat and his glasses. I had never seen him without his glasses before, except that time when we were playing in Clarkson's woods with Marion. He had a white mark over his nose where he had taken them off and it gave me the feeling that I could bash him easy. He gave them to a kid to look after and as the crowd started pushing the kid went: '*Mi-ind* his glasses!'

We both stepped forward to meet each other and put our fists up. We stood staring at each other and dancing round a bit like they do on the pictures, then I shot out my right hand to Garnett's chin but it missed and caught his shoulder. The next thing I knew was that his fist had caught me a stinging clout over the forehead. I was surprised and worried at the size of the blow and I began to notice, in a far-off sort of way, that he was a lot bigger than me and that his arms were thicker and longer.

I don't know how I got time to look at the people in the ring around us, but I did, and I noticed that I didn't even *know* most of them. Little Rayner was at the front shouting: 'Go it, Garno!' and this hurt me, don't ask me why. Ted was at the back, jumping up and down to get a good look.

I started trying to remember what people had told me about fighting. I knew you had to hit a man on his shoulders so as to weaken his arms, and another trick was to pretend to hit him in the belly and then when his arms went down, well you get him in the face instead. They didn't work. I hit Garno twice on his right shoulder and he didn't feel anything, and when I tried to go for his belly my own arms were down and he hit me on the lip. I could feel it swelling already and I heard the crowd go: 'Ohhhhh!' I suddenly realized that I had made a mistake and that Garno was tougher than I was and he was going to wipe the blinking floor with me and there was nothing I could do about it.

I remembered reading in the *Hotspur* or somewhere about all these boxers, they always hit with their left. I tried to hit Garno with my left hand but I couldn't aim it properly and I missed. Little Rayner started going: 'Cur, call this a fight!' One or two kids at the back had started their own little fights.

I started trying to look in Garno's eyes all the time. This was something else I remembered. If you look the other man in the eyes all the time, well you can tell what he's going to do.

You couldn't tell what blinking *Gar*no was going to do. He seemed surprised that I was staring at him all the time, and for a minute I thought he was going to start saying: 'Have you seen all?' His mouth was pursed up and he looked as though he was getting his mad up. Suddenly, for no reason at all as far as I could see, he went: 'Right! You've asked for it now!' and he started laying in to me. I started dancing round backwards like proper boxers do. There was a bump or a stone or something and I tripped over it and fell, sprawling. Little Rayner shouted: 'What you doing on the floor, man?' Garno stood over me, breathing through his mouth.

'Do you give in?' he said.

The question seemed cocky and unfair. I said: 'We haven't started yet!' I got up on my feet and he hit me with his fist in the face. I didn't fall this time but I turned round to stop him hitting me. I was all hunched up and almost cringing and I could feel his knuckles on the back of my head. Some kids were drifting away from the back of the crowd and that was even worse. Ted at the back started shouting: 'One—two—three—four, who—are—*we*—for—GARno!' Nobody took up the cry and he sounded silly.

Garno had stopped moving round the ring now. He just stood there and every time I came near him he hit me. He hit me in the lip again and it started bleeding.

We stood staring at each other, our fists clenched, breathing heavily. I said to the kid who had my coat: 'Get us my hanky,' because the blood was going down my chin.

The kid said: 'Clean your boots for fourpence.' He dropped my coat on the floor and started going: 'Yurrrks!' as though it were all over lice or something.

'Do you give in?' said Raymond Garnett.

I didn't answer him, I couldn't. Suddenly Garno lifted his hand and slapped me across the cheek. It wasn't with his fist, it was with his open hand. I had to bite into my bleeding lip to stop myself from crying. The tears came up into my eyes.

'*So-ock* him, man!' said Little Rayner.

'Do you give in?' said Raymond Garnett. He slapped me across the face again. I couldn't stop the tears rolling down my cheeks.

'Yer,' I muttered.

Garnett started dusting his hands together and said: 'Right, that's that, then!' And then from the back Ted shouted: 'He's still got his fists up, Garno!' Hurriedly I let my fists go and dropped my hands to my side. 'Do you want any more?' said Garno. 'No,' I said. 'Right,' he said again. 'That's that, then!'

He took his glasses from the kid who was holding them and put them on, pulling the wire up so that it went over his ears. He did not put his coat on but held it over his arm as he walked away. One or two kids patted him on the back and said: 'Good old you, man!' Nobody said anything to me and I picked my coat up off the floor and they began to drift away.

I walked across the field in the direction of Parkside. Once I thought I heard Little Rayner shouting after me: 'Laddy-lass!' but I could not be sure.

In the ditch at the side of the road two little girls were playing. They were only small. I did not know either of them. They were playing at nursery rhymes. *One, two, three four five, once I caught a fish alive. Then I let it go again.*

The second one replied: '*Why did you let it go?*'

'*Because it bit my finger so.*'.

Then both of them chanted together, laughing and giggling and sometimes stumbling over the words: '*Which finger did it bite? This little finger on the right?*'

Across the field, faintly, I could hear Little Rayner's voice again. This time there was no mistake about it, he was shouting: 'Laddy-lass.'

15

MY Auntie Betty was at the shops getting some
potatoes when I got home. I went up to the
hole at the top of our garden, but she had gone
and filled it in, like she always said she was going to do.
I went into the house and sat in the armchair trying to
read a comic, but my eyes were fixed on the same square
all the time, where Hungry Horace was taking a knife
and fork to a pie labelled 'PIE.' I thought to myself that
they didn't *la*bel pies with the word 'pie,' but I couldn't
take in the other squares. I was shaking all over and I
knew if my Aunt Betty started on at me I would start
crying.

She must have heard about the fight from Mrs
Theaker or somebody because when she came in she
didn't say anything, even though she must have noticed
my face. Only once, when we were having our tea and
I bit into some malt loaf and my split lip hurt and I
winced, she said: 'Yes, well that's what you get.' She
never mentioned the fight again.

The tight feeling was in my chest until half an hour
after tea. After that I found that I could sigh great gulps
of air and I began to feel better. I went out and I could
smell a wood fire somewhere. The air was crisp and
adventurous and I breathed deeply again and felt a
wave of happiness.

I could see no one in the street except Barbara

Monoghan and Kathleen Fawcett. They were sitting on Fawcett's gate. I went up to them and Barbara Monoghan said: 'You had a fight with Raymond Garnett today, didn't you?'

I said: 'Yer.'

'He beat you didn't he?'

'Only just,' I said.

They seemed friendly enough, but they were giggling over some blinking secret that they had, and that was the only reason they were talking to me.

'Don't you wish you knew where Marion Longbottom was?' said Kathleen Fawcett.

'No, why should I?' I said. I didn't want to see Marion with my split lip. I had finished writing the film magazine I had been doing for her, the Film Gazette, but I thought I might as well wait until my lip got better.

'We know where she is, don't we, Barbara?' said Kathleen Fawcett.

'Yer, but we're not telling him,' said Barbara.

'Don't want to know,' I said.

'Have we to tell him?' said Kathleen Fawcett.

'Have if he's coming to the tusky fields,' said Barbara.

'Why, what's up?' I said.

'Sky. Umbrellas when it's raining,' said Barbara. I followed them through Theaker's garden and into the tusky fields. There was nothing *else* to do. We sat down in a den we had made in the middle of the fields where we had flattened the big leaves down and we were hidden by the long rhubarb plants.

I broke off a stick of rhubarb and snapped it in two. The stick broke but not the skin, and I started to bend it backwards and forwards trying to make it give.

'Can't even break a stick of rhubarb,' said Barbara Monoghan.

I said: 'Where's Marion Longbottom, thought you were off to tell us?'

'Bet you wish you knew,' said Kathleen Fawcett.

I peeled the bloodshot skin off and began to eat the green ribbed rhubarb. The juice got in my lip and I winced and stood up, half crouching.

'You can see them if you wash the muck out of your eyes,' said Barbara Monoghan.

'See who?' I said.

I looked around the rhubarb fields. I was just in time to see a head bobbing down behind the leaves at the far end of the fields.

'Who, Big Rayner?' I said. I was sure it was him.

'Who do you think?' said Barbara Monoghan.

I sat down again, still looking over the leaves towards the top of the fields. Barbara Monoghan and Kathleen Fawcett didn't even look up.

'Hey, do you know what Mrs Theaker's first name is?' asked Barbara Monoghan.

'No, what?' said Kathleen.

'Have a guess.'

Across the fields I saw Big Rayner stand up, bent nearly double, and run across the fields in the direction of the Clerk of Works department. Marion Longbottom was just behind him. She was bent double as well, as she ran. They both thought they were hidden by the leaves.

'They call her Alice,' said Barbara Monoghan.

Big Rayner and Marion Longbottom reached the fence that divides the Clerk of Works department from the field where the den was that we were all in that time when Mrs Fawcett played pop. Instead of climbing over the fence they ducked under it.

'We can see you, so you needn't think we can't!' shouted Kathleen Fawcett suddenly. But neither she nor Barbara looked up nor showed any more interest.

'Have we to play truth or dare?' said Kathleen after a bit.

I didn't like truth or dare. Sooner or later it always got round to who goes out with who and kissing and that. I never said 'dare' in this game. I always said 'truth.'

'Truth or dare?' said Kathleen.

'Truth,' said Barbara Monoghan.

'Errrm—how many times have you been out with Big Rayner?'

'What, by himself?'

'Yer,' said Kathleen.

'Errr—once to the Tivoli one Saturday afternoon, once down to Clarkson's woods. No, twice. Three times, altogether,' said Barbara.

I was looking over at the fence where Marion and Big Rayner had gone, but I could not see them any more. This was the first time I had ever seen them together. Marion always said she didn't like the big lads, and I know her mother had told her to keep away from Big Rayner.

She was wearing her velvet dress, the one that looked like our tablecloth. It wasn't a very nice *dress*, because it was all old and bits of the velvet had worn off, but I liked it because you always think of somebody in a certain thing and I always thought of Marion in this velvet dress. Not the night before but the night before that we had made some furniture out of old matchboxes in their house, using drawing pins for the drawer handles. Marion hadn't seemed much interested.

'Truth or dare?' said Barbara Monoghan.

'Truth,' said Kathleen.

'No, dare,' said Barbara.

'No, truth. You had truth so I'm having truth.'

'How many times have you been in the tusky fields with our kid?' said Barbara Monoghan.

'Aw, not answering that,' said Kathleen.

'Well dare, then,'

'All right, dare.'

'Dare you to ask him something,' Barbara Monoghan nodded towards me and began whispering in Kathleen's ear. They both started giggling. I started peeling the skins off a rhubarb leaf and pretended not to take any notice.

'Truth or dare,' said Kathleen Fawcett.

'Truth,' I said.

'Well what—kkkkkksh!' She made a lot of giggly false starts before she asked the question that Barbara Monoghan had whispered to her. 'What colour knick-knacks does Marion Longbottom wear?'

Only Barbara could think up a question like that.

'Blue,' I guessed. I thought they *meant* me to guess.

'Ha, he knows!' shouted Barbara Monoghan. 'Huh, I'll tell, don't you worry!' she cackled.

'Ask him how he knows,' said Kathleen Fawcett.

'I-I-I was only guessing,' I said. I could feel myself going red.

'Yer, bet you were!' said Barbara. 'What colour ones does Kathleen Fawcett wear, then?'

'So, Barbara Monoghan!' said Kathleen. I was trying hard for some excuse to get away. Barbara Monoghan started pulling her dress up and pulling it back again, very quickly, over her knees, with Kathleen shouting: 'Blue! Brown!' It was the kind of stupid thing they were always doing.

'Truth or dare?' said Barbara Monoghan, when she had finished acting about.

'I've had it once!' I went.

'Ah, well, you've got to have another. Truth or dare?'

'Dare,' I said. I couldn't say truth again.

'Dare you to kiss Kathleen Fawcett.'

'Oo, you wait, Barbara Monoghan!' said Kathleen. I didn't know what to do. I didn't want to kiss Kathleen Fawcett, and the way she had said: 'Oo, you wait!' to Barbara made me think she didn't want me to. But if I didn't they would laugh at me. I suddenly drew in my breath and said: 'Listen!' in a hoarse voice.

'What's up?'

'My Aunt Betty's shouting me.'

'Caw, trying to get out of it!' cried Barbara Monoghan.

'No, listen!' I stood up and cupped my hands to my face and shouted: 'Just coming!' across the fields. '*I* can't hear nobody,' said Kathleen. 'Want to wash your ears out, then,' I said. 'They're sprouting cabbages.'

I set off through the rhubarb leaves with Barbara and Kathleen shouting after me: '*We'll* tell Mrs Longbottom! Tea-cher's pe-et! You wait!'

'And you needn't go to our kid's fire!' shouted Barbara Monoghan. I could still smell the wood smoke, so it must have been Mono's fire in their garden.

'I'm not *off* to it. My Auntie Betty wants me!' I shouted back.

'Yer, *bet* she does!' called Kathleen Fawcett.

I went back through Theaker's garden and into

Coronation Grove. The wood smell was very strong there and I walked up the street as far as Mono's. I stood by their gate for a few seconds and then walked into the garden and along the side path to the back garden.

They were all sitting on bricks round a fire, melting lead from some piping they had pinched and moulding it into squares in an old Oxo tin. My heart sank because Ted and Raymond Garnett were there, besides Mono, Little Rayner and a few more.

As I walked over towards them Little Rayner started singing: 'Here comes the bride, fifty inches wide!' Raymond Garnett said nothing. Mono stood up and said: 'Who told you *you* could come in?'

I said: 'Nobody.' It was a law that you could go in anybody's garden if they had a fire.

'Do you want another fight, or something?' asked Little Rayner. I didn't reply, but stood on the fringe of the fire.

'Cos I'll give you one if you do,' said Little Rayner. He was small and thin, not like their kid, and he never fought anybody.

'*He-e* couldn't knock the skin off a rice pudding,' said Ted.

'Have we to set on him?' said Little Rayner.

'Cuh, seven against one!' I said.

'We'll take you on one at a time if you want,' said Raymond Garnett. It was the first time he had spoken. He had changed in his voice. He sounded sure of himself and his voice had got the harsh rasp of Mono and Big Rayner to it now.

Little Rayner picked up a stone and held it up ready to throw.

'Dance!' he said.

'You throw that if you dare!' I said.

'Why, what will you do?' asked Mono mockingly.

'Dance!' said Little Rayner.

He threw the pebble at my feet and picked up another. Ted picked up a piece of slate and joined in. 'Dance!' he said. Nearly all of them had stones. I had to jump up and down to get out of the way of the stones that they were lobbing at my ankles.

'Gi-ive over?' I shouted. 'Lay off!'

'Go down to Uncle Mad's and he'll kiss you better!' said Ted. 'Won't he, Garno?'

'Don't *you* start!' said Raymond Garnett.

Mono came up to me and started pushing at me with his elbows.

'Go on, scram!' he said.

'Won't if I don't want to,' I said.

'*Ho-op* it, college cad!' shouted Ted.

'Cur, just cos I got ten out of ten in composition!' I sneered back at him. Me and Ted had always been rivals in composition. We had to write a composition about a day in the life of a sheep, and I had written it as though I was the sheep and I got ten out of ten.

'*Ho-op* it, wolf cub!' said Mono.

'Yer, well I'm not in the boy sprouts like some people,' I said

Little Rayner put up his two fingers in a mock salute. 'I promise to do my best!' he went in a squeaking voice. He had chucked out of the wolf cubs.

'Dance!' said Ted. I turned round and walked out of the garden. Little Rayner sang after me: 'Here comes the bride, fifty inches wide!' 'No this is it,' I heard

Raymond Garnett say. 'Here comes the bride, with a bla-ack eye!'

I walked down Coronation Grove, feeling my split lip swollen and numb. Near the end of our street I began to straighten my back and hold my arms at my sides, curving my fingers a bit, like Big Rayner did. I pushed out my split lip and glared round me.

At the corner of Royal Park Crescent and Carnegie Road a couple of kids I didn't know sat on a sandbin, staring at me. I pushed my lip out a bit more and shouted: 'What are you staring at?' They didn't say anything but just kept on staring.

'Do you *want* it?' I said. 'Because you're going to get it.' Neither of them moved.

I went up Carnegie Road, down Wharfedale Avenue and along Wharfedale Gardens. I sucked my sore lip back in and let my shoulders drop. Uncle Mad's fire engine wasn't outside his door, but I knew which house it was. I leaned on the gate-post for a while and then I went up the broken path to the front door. I knocked at the door. It was one of these long brass knockers, fastened on to the letter box. It echoed through the house as though I were knocking at the door of an empty barn.

16

THERE was no reply at first.

Through the frosted glass I could see the hall and the partly-open door that led into the scullery. It was very still inside, like a house where all the people are on holiday and have been for a long time. I knocked again.

I began to feel silly in case anybody out in the street was watching me knocking. I had a little red notebook in my pocket, so I took it out and drew back a few steps from the door and looked up at the window, pretending to be counting something, and pretending to write it down in this book. I didn't have a pencil but I tried to look as if I had.

Then I walked round to the side of the house, closed one eye and held my arms out along the side of the house as if I was measuring *that* as well. I pretended to write this down too. Then I walked back and knocked on the door again, using the code knock that I used to have with Ted.

Heard a scuffling noise and somebody shouted: 'Hullo?'

It was not Uncle Mad's voice, it was a kid's voice.

I put my face to the crack of the door and said: 'Is Raymond Garnett in?' It was the first thing that came into my head.

The voice said: 'Who?' I said: 'Raymond Garnett. That kid.'

The voice said: 'Don't know him, don't want to.'
There was another scuffling noise and whoever it was
seemed to go away. I knocked on the door again, this
time braying on the glass with my knuckles.

This time another voice answered me. It was still a
kid's voice. It said: '*Ho-op* it, kid!'

I put my face to the crack of the door again and said:
'Let us in, man.'

'What for?'

'Cos for.'

The voice said: 'If you want Garno he isn't here.'

I said: 'I know. I've got something to tell Uncle Mad.'

'What have you got to tell him?'

'*Some*thing.'

'Well you can tell him next time.' The house went
quiet again. I knocked on the door again, then I took
out my notebook and measured up the house again.
Then I turned round and walked down the path.

Just as I got to the gate the door opened a bit and a
kid shouted: 'You can come in if you want to.' I looked
round and saw it was Spenco, one of the kids me and
Garno went down to the quarries with on Uncle Mad's
fire engine that time. One of the kids out of the Catholic
school.

I turned back and went inside. I had never been in
Uncle Mad's before. The hall was blinking empty. The
floorboards were bare and there was no carpet down on
the stairs and the well where the doormat should have
been had all dust in it. A voice shouted: '*In* here, man!'
and I went into the living-room.

It was like Fawcett's, only worse. There were no
curtains up at the windows for a start. One of the
windows was broken and it had been stuffed up with

an old corn-flakes box squashed flat. *These* floorboards were bare as well. There was no furniture in the room except an old table and a broken-down old sofa.

The three kids were sitting on the sofa, all trying to look as though they weren't doing anything like you do when you're in somebody's house and his mother comes in. The three kids were Spenco, Peggo and young Gin'er, the same kids that we'd been on Uncle Mad's fire engine with.

They all gave me a funny look.

'Who gave you your busted lip?' said Spenco.

'Kid in our school,' I said. I was going to tell them about my fight with Raymond Garnett, but they didn't seem interested.

'What school do you go to?' asked Peggo, the one with his leg in irons.

'Parkside,' I said.

'Cuh, we go to the Catholic school, don't we, Spenco?'

'Yer,' said Spenco.

'What's it like at your school?' I asked.

'It's all right, man,' said Peggo.

'Do you get taught by them nuns?'

'Yer.'

'Do they hit you?'

'No. Father Thomas does, though.'

'Sister Clare hits *me*,' said young Gin'er. It was the first time he had spoken. He had been trying to hold his breath to see how long he could do it for.

'She hits me as well,' said Peggo.

The sofa they were sitting on looked as if it had been thrown out on bonfire night. It only had three legs and the springs were hanging out all over the shop. One of the arms had broken off and it had been left just leaning up against the blinking sofa. There were bits of fluff out of the sofa all over the floor. There was nothing else on the floor except a piece of chalk, ground into the floor-boards by somebody's foot, and the lid off a Mansion Polish tin. On the table there was half a bottle of milk and a tin of Rowntree's cocoa, the label ripped half-way down the tin, but there was nothing else.

'Where's Uncle Mad?' I asked.

'Gone out,' said Spenco. 'What have you got to tell him?'

'*N*othing,' I said.

'You came down to the quarries with us that time, didn't you, thingy?' said young Gin'er.

'Yer.'

'You haven't been in here before, though, have you?' said Peggo.

'No.'

'We're always coming, aren't we, Peggo?' said Spenco.

'Does he let you stop in the house when he goes out?' I asked.

'Yer, you just walk in,' said Spenco.

'Can anybody walk in?'

'Can if they want,' said Spenco. 'Have a look round if you want, man.'

'Can you go upstairs?' I said.

'Yer, course you can,' said Spenco. He seemed to be in charge. He got up and all four of us went up the steps. I wouldn't go up at first but they all said it was all right, so I followed them up. There were three rooms on the landing. The doors of two of them were open. The third was closed, closed on purpose as though it had been locked, although there was no lock on the door. Don't

151

ask me why, but it reminded me of that blinking Bluebeard story in the Fifth Reader.

We went into one of the rooms, the smallest one. It was empty except for a pile of rags, but the room looked worse than our playground. There were chalk marks everywhere. The floor was marked out for circular hop-scotch—where you write your name in a square every time you've been round, and nobody else can go in your square—and somebody had been rubbing it in with their foot.

The walls were all marked in squiggly lines where somebody had been running round holding a crayon against the wall. There were people's initials all over the show as well.

I burst out: 'Hey, look at all this, man!' •

'What's up, he won't say anything,' said Spenco.

'Has he *seen* it?'

'Course he has. He's all right, is Uncle Mad.'

'And doesn't he play pop?'

'Course he doesn't.'

Young Gin'er said: 'I'm off to count up to a million.'

We went into the second room. That was empty as well, except for an old wheel on the floor. It looked like an old cartwheel. It lay lopsided on its hub.

'That's *our* wheel,' said Peggo.

'Does he let you keep it here?'

'Yer.'

Spenco was over at the window. He clambered up on the sill and pressed up against the window with his arms stretched out. 'I've jumped *out* of this window,' he said.

'So have *I*, man, so you needn't swank!' said Peggo. I didn't see how he could have done with his leg in irons, but I didn't say anything. For all I knew he might have broke his leg jumping out of the window, and that's why he had to have this iron on it.

'I've never jumped out of it,' said young Gin'er. He had stopped counting up to a million because nobody was taking any notice. He didn't look as though he would dare jump out of the ground-floor window, even. He was too small and pale and he wore braces instead of a belt. Spenco and Peggo were tough, but not in the same way as Big Rayner and them.

We went out of that room and stood on the landing. I looked at the door that was closed.

'You can't go in there,' said Spenco.

'Can't you?'

'No.'

'*I've* been in,' said young Gin'er.

'What's in it, man?' I asked him.

'Nothing. It's only an old bed.'

'Who said you could go in?' asked Spenco.

'Nobody. I just went in,' said young Gin'er.

'Have *we* to go in?' said Peggo.

'No, man,' said Spenco. Peggo wasn't bothered. He went back into the room where we had just been and and shouted: 'Hey, rolling that wheel down them stairs!'

'Oo, yer, man!' called Spenco. 'We roll that wheel downstairs sometimes,' he said to me.

Him and Peggo got hold of the wheel and pulled it to the top of the stairs. Young Gin'er didn't help. He seemed frightened.

'*No-o*, man! They'll hear!' he shouted.

Peggo and Spenco took no notice. They got hold of the cartwheel, one on each side.

'One to get ready, two to get steady, three to be o-OFF!'

They let go of the wheel and it shot down the stairs. It missed the first three stairs out and landed on the fourth. It did not roll cleanly down the stairs but scraped against the wall. It landed just at the bottom of the staircase. I bet you could hear the clatter a mile off.

'*You-ou* can't throw for toffee, man!' sneered Spenco. '*Let's* have a go!'

He ran downstairs after the wheel, Peggo following after him going more slowly because of his leg. Gin'er called out: 'They'll *hear* you, man! I'm *tell*ing you!' He was scared stiff. I was feeling a bit frightened as well, standing there at the top of the stairs. I didn't like being upstairs in somebody else's house because my Auntie Betty always said you hadn't go, and I kept listening for somebody coming.

Spenco and Peggo dragged the wheel back up to the top of the stairs. 'Mind out!' shouted Spenco. 'Let a *man* have a go!'

This time he rolled the wheel by himself.

It toppled smoothly down the stairs, not touching the wall or the bannister, making a bump on each stair as it fell and gathering speed until it crashed with a great blinking thud against the door at the bottom. I thought the door was going through for a minute.

Young Gin'er was nearly crying. 'Aw, *gi-ive* up, man!' he begged. His fright seemed to make the others want to make more noise than ever and they started doing Indian yodels and shouting: '*Al*-li-*squash*er!' as if they were playing hiddy.

'It's not me if anyone comes!' cried young Gin'er. I was trying not to take any notice but I kept walking quickly up and down the landing because I suddenly wanted to go to the lavatory.

'Hey, rolling it off that table!' called out Spenco. They piled downstairs and got the wheel on the table in the living-room. Me and young Gin'er went in after them. They started dropping the wheel on the floor off the table.

'*You-ou*'-*ll* bash the blinking floorboards in!' went young Gin'er, white with fright.

I said: '*Shu-ut* up, man!' pretending to be on their side. I was scared silly. They kept dropping the wheel off the table and shouting: '*Al*-li-*squash*er!'

All of a sudden young Gin'er called out in a hoarse, frightened whisper: 'Hey, listen!'

'Bodibodibodibo!' yelled Spenco, just shouting for the love of it.

'*List*en, man! There's somebody at the door!'

The front door knocker banged through the noise. I whispered: 'Is it the feller?'

'No, he comes straight in,' said Spenco. 'I bet it's my mother.'

'Hey, what if it's mine?' whispered young Gin'er.

'*I-i-it*'s not yours. She never comes here,' said Spenco. The knocking went on.

'Will she go away?' I asked.

'Will she heckers like,' said Spenco. He went over to the window and strained himself to look at the door outside. 'Yer, it's my mother.'

He went into the hall and shouted: 'Just coming!'

A woman's voice bawled out: 'What have I told you about other people's houses!'

'*We-er*'*e* not doing anything!' called Spenco. He opened the door and called back to us: '*Co-o-me* on!' as though we were holding him back.

A woman in an apron was at the door. She had it

rolled up to her waist like a woodwork apron. She hit Spenco over the head as he ducked past her. 'And you keep out of there in future!' she screamed after him. She took no notice of us. We trooped out after her.

She caught up with Spenco at the gate and took hold of his arm and started hitting him. 'How—many—more—times—have I—to tell—*you*?'

'*O*mmi!' shouted Spenco. 'My sore arm! Get o-o-off!'

Peggo shut the front door behind him. We left the cartwheel in the living-room.

17

USED to go to Uncle Mad's a lot after that, never telling the others and always making up lies to say where I'd been. I used to say I'd been down to the school clinic and all over so my Auntie Betty wouldn't find out.

Peggo, Spenco and young Gin'er were nearly always there, one or other of them, and sometimes Uncle Mad was there himself. He never took any notice of us, except when we passed him in the doorway and then he would go: 'Gr-*qua*-ack' or 'Cuit cuit cuit cuit!' as per usual. He never seemed to mind us being in his house, in fact it might have been somebody *else's* house for all he cared. We used to write on the walls and jump up and down and that but he never said anything. We never knocked at the door, just used to walk straight in. Sometimes we would sit on this broken-down old sofa and watch Uncle Mad doing some job I could never get the point of, like beating a condensed milk tin out into a flat sheet of tin. Spenco used to be always going: 'Let's have a go, Uncle Mad!' but whatever he was doing, Uncle Mad never took any notice except to look up and go: 'Grr-quack!'

Other times we would go up into the empty rooms upstairs and chalk or play at rolling this wheel. We never rolled it down the stairs when Uncle Mad was there, but I bet he wouldn't have said anything if we had.

Anyway, one afternoon I finished up going straight round to Uncle Mad's straight after school. I wasn't going to, always used to wait till I'd had my tea, but where it was, Marion Longbottom started getting right funny. Marion was all right, but you never knew where you were with her. Sometimes she would want to play houses in their back garden, and other times she would say that playing houses was cissy, and she would go off on her own. Anyway, today I thought I would go off down to their school gates and meet her coming out of school. Why I went to meet her was, I'd made this film book for her out of pages torn of my Auntie Betty's co-op book, and I wanted to give it to her. Marion was dead crackers about the pictures and I had made this Film Gazette by cutting out all the photos of these film stars out of that Picturegoer book that comes out and sticking them in. I'd already told her it was finished and she was dead pleased only somehow I never got chance to give it to her, because she was never in when I called for her. So I thought I would go round to their school gates and wait for her.

The girls' school was in the same building as us, only they had a different gate further up. I walked up to the gates of the girls' department and waited outside. All the blinking lasses were coming out so I started pretending to be jumping up on the wall and getting hold of the railings. I had this film book in my pocket and I was going to give it to Marion when she came out.

After a bit I saw her coming out with about three other lasses. They were all carrying like these blue bags that they put their raffia-work in. I stood on the low wall and got hold of the railings above it and started swinging back with my arms, seeing how far I could get without letting go. Marion could see me, and I thought she would come up and say something. But instead she walks straight past and starts giggling with these other lasses. I heard one of them say: 'Looks like a monkey, want to give it some monkey nuts,' but I didn't know whether it was Marion or not who spoke, and even if it was I didn't know whether she was talking about me.

I thought she couldn't have seen me so I got down and started walking behind them. They still didn't take any notice, so I thought I'd start pretending to be looking for somebody. I cupped my hands to my mouth and shouted: 'Mono!' It was the first name that came into my head.

Still didn't take any notice. I started walking faster until I caught up with them. Marion was on the outside and as I reached her I said: 'Hiya, Marion,' trying to speak as if it was an everyday thing to be walking past her, but I could feel myself going red.

Marion muttered: 'Hiya.' I walked on until I was just past her, then I took the film book out of my pocket and held it out to her to take as she caught me up. 'There's that film book,' I said. Marion screwed her face up as though she didn't know what I was talking about and went: 'You *what*?'

I said: 'Don't you want it?'

She said: 'Want what, don't know what you're on about.'

I said: 'That film book, thought you *want*ed it.'

None of the other three lasses said anything. They were all too busy trying to keep their faces straight. 'Not mine,' said Marion, and I knew she didn't want my film book any more. They walked past me again. I called out: 'Have I to call for you tonight?' Marion didn't answer, but one of the other lasses turned round and said: 'Says you needn't bother.'

I let them go. I held the film book in my hand and looked down at the brown photograph of this cowboy glued on to the front page. It was all crumpled and there were black marks where the glue had got smudged. Marion and these other lasses were just going past our school gates. I saw Big Rayner and another kid standing there, leaning on the railings. Big Rayner shouted: '*Co*-ome on!' at the lasses, and him and this other kid walked off with Marion and the other lasses walking behind them.

I walked slowly so I wouldn't catch them up, holding my film book and slowly peeling off this picture of the cowboy. It wouldn't come clean off but tore, leaving a sort of white fuzz where his head had been and leaving the picture of his head curled up in my hand.

Instead of walking up past our school I turned off and went down Park Avenue, and along Wharfedale Gardens towards Uncle Mad's. I was supposed to be going to the barber's that night but I had spent the money, and that was why I didn't go straight home.

I got to Uncle Mad's and just walked in through the front door, as per usual. It was too early for the others to be there, I suppose. It was very quiet and there was nobody about. I shouted: 'Spenco!' then 'Peggo!' and then 'Uncle Ma-ad!' but there was no reply from anyone.

I went to the bottom of the stairs and shouted: 'Is there anybody in?' Then I began to climb the stairs. I went up and looked in the room where we had put chalk marks on the walls. The hopscotch mark was still on the floor and there were still these brown squiggly lines all round the walls. But they looked old, unused, as though no one had ever lived there.

I went into the second room and the cartwheel was lying on the floor, quietly, as though it had never moved, ever. It was very quiet. Suddenly I started thinking of a dream I sometimes had, where I went into this house and it was dark and there was something at the top of the stairs, and I tried to run away only I couldn't move. My back started tingling and when I looked at my arm, it had gone all gooseflesh.

I went out on to the landing and looked down the stairs. I had left the door open and I could see the path outside and a bit of Uncle Mad's fire engine and there was a woman walking past up the street. I felt glad. I went back along the landing. There was this closed door that we had never opened. I looked at it and my heart started thumping and I thought for a minute of this blinking Bluebeard story, where he has this locked room full of women's heads. Then I walked up to the door and put my fingers on the handle and turned it. The door was unlocked. I drew a deep breath and started to push it open.

All of a sudden I heard this creak on the staircase. I closed the door again, but whoever it was, they must have heard me. I went back into the little room and picked up the cartwheel and stood by the window, pretending to be counting the spokes but hoping someone would pass by in the street outside and see me standing there.

The creak turned into a footstep and someone was

coming up the stairs. They paused, and walked along the landing.

It was Uncle Mad. He stopped at the doorway and looked in. Didn't ask me what I thought I was doing, just went: 'Grr-qua-ack!' and walked on towards the room with the closed door. He looked funny somehow or other, but don't ask me how.

I said: 'Hiya, Uncle Mad! Is it all right for me to play with this wheel?'

He went: 'Grr-qua-ack!' again, but that was all. I walked to the door and saw that he had gone inside the other room. The door was partly open. I could just get a glimpse of an oval toffee tin on the mantelpiece with some string coming out of it, and the corner of a bed. It was a brass bedstead with the top knob dented. There were no blankets on it, only striped ticking.

It was the striped ticking that frightened me. I walked downstairs as fast I could without running. The door was closed now, the outside door, and I wondered whether to go out or go into the living-room. I went into the living-room and sat on the old sofa where I could see out of the big window. There was a fire and a poker sticking into it to warm up.

I heard Uncle Mad coming downstairs and he came into the room carrying the end of a box, just the thick part that they have for the ends.

He went: 'Cuit cuit cuit!' at me and winked. He didn't look funny now, just ordinary, that's all. He knelt down on the floor and took the poker out of the fire. It was red hot. He started boring holes in this piece of wood.

'What are you doing, Uncle Mad?' I said. I knew he wouldn't tell me. He was always doing things like that and you never knew why. He was making these holes right through the wood in lines, about an inch apart.

'*Tell* us what you're doing,' I said.

'Grr-qua-ack!' He stuck the poker back in the fire and started blowing the burnt away out of the holes he had made.

Can't remember what happened next, but I do know he got up and stretched and then he turned and faced me. He sort of smiled, I think. I said: 'Are you waiting for it getting red hot again?' He came back and sat on the sofa at the side of me and shut his eyes.

We sat like that for a few minutes. Then all of a sudden Uncle Mad went: 'Grr-quack!' and grabbed hold of my knee for a second. I started laughing and he shut his eyes again. Then he went: 'Qua-ack!' and grabbed my knee for the second time. There were all warts on his hand.

I laughed but I did not really like it. For one thing, when he went: 'Grr-qua-ack' it was all right, but when he just went: 'Qu-ack!' like that, it was different. It was like these uncles who are always getting you in the stomach and going: 'Kitsi-kitsi-kitsi-kitsi-kitsi!'

Uncle Mad lay back again and closed his eyes. This time he pretended to be asleep and moved his hand without opening his eyes. Then just as suddenly as before he grabbed my knee again and went: 'Qua-ack!'

I laughed uncomfortably and said: 'Your *poker's* getting hot!' Then he did it again, and this time instead of letting go he kept hold of my blinking kneecap. I tried to shove his hand away and I felt these warts, all rough. He wouldn't move it. I didn't know what he was playing at but I didn't like it and I got up. He made a sudden grab for me and this time he didn't make any noise and I knew he wasn't playing. I dragged myself away and staggered backwards over to the fireplace.

And then Uncle Mad spoke. Speaking in a high-pitched, squeaky voice as though he was taking Mickey Mouse off he went: '*Who's been sleeping in MY bed?*' out of the Three Bears. It was the first time I had ever heard him speak. You could tell it wasn't his real voice, he was just putting it on, and that frightened me more than anything.

I ran for the door. Uncle Mad squeaked after me: '*I, said the sparrow, with my bow and arrow.*' The living-room door was partly open and I ran into it. I stumbled round it and grabbed at the doorknob of the front door. The Yale lock was on. I started fumbling at it and sniffling to myself. Uncle Mad didn't move from the sofa, but he was doing a thing out of the Three Little Pigs: '*I'll huff and I'll puff and I'll BLOW the house down.*' Great billows of smoke were coming from the poker in the fire, but he didn't move.

I got the door open and I ran out and left it open. I breathed in the fresh air and got at the side of a woman who was walking up the street. Looking round I saw Uncle Mad staring out of the window at me. I started running and half-crying at the same time, gurgling to myself as I ran. I ran all the way up Wharfedale Avenue and along Carnegie Road to the bottom of our street. I kept looking back and each time I thought I saw him after me.

I couldn't run any further and I walked up our street, looking back all the time.

Up round our lamp-post they were all playing hiddy.

I felt glad as I passed Little Rayner who was hiding behind Longbottom's gate. Ted shouted, trying to sound as if it didn't matter one way or the other: 'Do you want a game?'

I said: 'No, man. I've to get my tea. I've just been to the barber's.' I went in.

18

THE next night Marion Longbottom got lost.

It must have been about six o'clock at night when Mrs Longbottom came out of their door and started asking everybody where she was. Nobody had seen her.

'She might be watching that Punch and Judy feller up near our school,' said Barbara Monoghan. 'There was a crowd there last time I saw him.'

'I'll Punch and Judy her when I get hold of her,' said Mrs Longbottom. 'She knows she's to go to the fish-shop on a Friday night.'

I was sitting on our gate. The others were playing hopscotch. I didn't know where Marion was, and I didn't blinking well care. Didn't worry me whether she got into cop it or not. Mrs Longbottom started shouting down the street: 'Marion! Marion!' After a bit she said: 'When I get my hands on that little madam she'll know about it.'

She went in. After a bit Mr Longbottom came out in his shirt-sleeves. Thought he was going to start telling us all jokes like he always did. I shouted: 'We haven't found them treacle mines yet, Mr Longbottom!' but he didn't seem to hear me. He started asking everybody where Marion was. Nobody knew. He went back in.

Barbara Monoghan and Kathleen Fawcett were up near our gate. They started nudging each other. 'Have

I to tell him?' Kathleen said. Barbara said: 'No, you'll get her into cop it.' Kathleen went: 'I don't care, I'm off to tell him.'

Mr and Mrs Longbottom came out again. This time they were together. Kathleen Fawcett took a step down the street and shouted: 'Mr Longbottom, are you looking for your Marion?'

Mr Longbottom came out of their gate and walked up the street towards them.

'Cos she hasn't been to school all afternoon,' said Kathleen. 'Has she, Barbara?'

'No, cos Miss Carson wanted to know where she was, didn't she?' said Barbara.

'I thought you said she was watching that Punch and Judy?' shouted Mrs Longbottom up the street.

'Well she might have been, but she wasn't at school,' went Barbara. 'You ask Queenie Davis. She's in their class as well.'

Mr Longbottom didn't say anything. He just went back in.

'She won't half get into cop it, now,' said Barbara.

'Serves her right, shouldn't be so stuck up,' said Kathleen.

A bit later Mr Longbottom came out again. This time he wore his cap and coat. Mrs Longbottom was with him, wearing the old black coat she wore when she went shopping.

Mrs Longbottom shouted out to Kathleen Fawcett: 'If she comes back, tell her to go to your mother's and stop there till we get back.'

They polled off up the street. I watched them come past. I shouted out to Mrs Longbottom: 'Mrs Longbottom!' She shouted back: 'What, love?'

I said: 'I'm sorry for shouting out at you that time.'

She didn't stop or say anything, just looked as if she didn't know what I was talking about.

I said: 'When me and Ted were shouting out at you that time.'

She said: 'You'll have to tell me another time, love.' I didn't know whether it was all right or not. She went off up the street with Mr Longbottom. We watched them go. They went past our house, past Monoghan's, and into Rayner's. We saw them go into Rayner's gate. Little Rayner was with us, but Big Rayner wasn't.

Little Rayner said: 'Hey, they're off in our house. I'm off to pelt after them.' He ran off up the street. Mono, he was there as well, he shouted after him: 'Bet *you* know where she is, young Rayno!'

They had all stopped playing hopscotch by now. They all stood round the lamp-post or sat on the causeway edge. I sat on our gate. My Auntie Betty came out and asked me what was up, and after a bit other people came out as well.

Soon Little Rayner came running down the street again, shouting. We couldn't hear what he was talking about at first but as he came nearer we could hear him bawling out: 'She's with Uncle Mad! She's with Uncle Mad!' He got up as far as the lamp-post and stopped for breath and then, still panting, he said: 'Cur, I bet she doesn't half get brayed. Our kid says she was with Uncle Mad this dinnertime. They were heading up towards the park.'

The women in the street started talking together in little groups, speaking softy so we would not hear them.

My Auntie Betty shouted at me: 'And don't you go past that lamp-post!' Mrs Fawcett shouted out to

Kathleen: 'Get in that house this minute!' A small crowd of people gathered round Longbottom's gate. After a bit Mr and Mrs Longbottom came down the street. Mrs Longbottom was nearly crying. Mr Longbottom was shouting: 'I'll break every bone in his bloody body! I will! I'll swing for him!' He must have been talking about Uncle Mad.

Mr Theaker and Mr Fawcett were standing outside in their shirt-sleeves. They had just come home from work. Mr Longbottom shouted: 'Are you coming down? It's not the first time he's had kids in that house!'

Mr Theaker, still in his shirt-sleeves, set off with Mr Longbottom. Mr Fawcett shouted: 'I'm looking after my own. I bet *she's* been down there as well.' He turned round and started braying their Kathleen over the head. The two men, Mr Longbottom and Mr Theaker, set off down the street. Here and there a man left one of the gates and joined up with them.

Mrs Longbottom had been talking to my Auntie Betty. My Auntie Betty went in and got her coat, then she said: 'I'm just going with Mrs Longbottom. Don't you move out of this street.'

They set off up Coronation Grove. I watched them out of sight, then I started off going the other way, the way Mr Longbottom and Mr Theaker had gone.

Mrs Fawcett shouted after me: 'I thought your Auntie said you hadn't to move out of this street?'

I said: '*I'm* only going to the house shop!' We always went to the house shop when the other shops were closed. I said I was going there.

'Well you don't go any further!' shouted Mrs Fawcett. Blinking nosey-parker. I walked as far as the house shop at the corner of Royal Park Crescent, then I started running. I ran into Carnegie Road, and far up the road I could see the group of men walking in the direction of Uncle Mad's. There were about eight or nine of them now. One of them was carrying a stick.

I slowed down and gave them a chance to get into Wharfedale Avenue. A lot of people had come to the doors to watch them going past. I set my face so that I could look sad and I started limping so they would know I couldn't keep up with the others.

By the time I got into Wharfedale Gardens they were all standing outside Uncle Mad's gate. The fire engine was gone. There was a big dirty patch on the ground where it had been, like that time it used to be up on the concrete path near the slag heaps. I was just in time to see Mr Longbottom and Mr Theaker coming out. Mr Theaker carried the cartwheel that had been in the room upstairs.

'There's that wheel,' he said to the others. 'I've always wondered where that got to.' He threw it down in the front garden and left it there.

From across the road a woman shouted: 'If you're looking for Mr Sissons, he's been out all afternoon.'

Mr Longbottom shouted: 'I don't know what his bloody name is. He's got my young 'un with him!'

'Oh, he's always taking other people's kids for rides,' the woman said. 'I tell mine to keep away.'

Suddenly Mr Longbottom seemed to go blinking crackers. He picked up the cartwheel from where it lay and threw it, so that it spun like a piece of slate on a lake and crashed up against the window. It did not go through the window. One pane went through altogether; two or three others cracked. The wheel fell in the bed of irises below the window. Nobody tried to stop Mr Longbottom.

'I'll bloody swing for him! I will!' he said.

The woman across the road shouted: 'He goes getting stones up in the park if you want him.'

'She's not been at school all afternoon,' bawled Mr Longbottom. 'We've only just got word.'

They set off again, past the clinic and up Park Avenue. I stood outside Uncle Mad's for a bit. I wanted to go in but I daren't. I limped off after the men, in the direction of the park.

It was like Tattoo Day down in the park. Nearly all Coronation Grove was there, some trooping down the steep road into the park, some poking about in the rhododendrons, shouting for each other across the great green space.

Down near the swings, in the big wooden shelter, my Auntie Betty sat resting with a woman I didn't know. I shouted over: 'Auntie Be-e-tty!'

She shouted: 'I thought I told you not to come down here!'

I said: 'I'm just off looking for Marion.'

She shouted: 'You're just off looking for nobody. You get back home, and look sharp!'

I said: 'Mr Longbottom said I could come.'

'It doesn't matter what Mr Longbottom says. It's what I say!'

I said: 'Well, Mono and Raymond Garnett and them's all down!'

'It doesn't matter who's down or who's up. You get back home!'

I could tell by the way she spoke that she didn't mean it, because all the others were down in the park as well. I walked off towards the lake. My Auntie Betty shouted: 'Do you hear me?' and I shouted back: 'I'm *go*ing!' Mr Longbottom and Mr Theaker were talking to one of the park rangers down by the lake.

I walked behind the wooden shelter and through these woods that lead on to Parkside quarries the back way, where we went getting stones with Uncle Mad that day. Some people were down there, beating through the ferns with sticks. I didn't know any of them. There was a policeman talking to a woman and writing it down in a black book. I wished I'd got one.

I walked through the woods and over the low wall that led on to the quarries. From there I could see right across the park, the people searching and talking together in groups. I pretended to be the boss and started ordering people around. There was no one near the quarries to hear me.

The green blackberries were just turning in colour around the quarries. It was getting a little cold, and now it began to grow dusky because the dark nights were coming. I wondered why nobody was looking in the quarries. I shivered a little, and started going: 'All right, you work round that way and report back to me.' There was no one to listen. I wished there had of been, because I was a bit frightened.

I slithered down the dry sandy slope, getting it on my trousers like that day I came with Garno, getting stones for Uncle Mad. I daren't go down to the bottom of the quarry. I stood half-way down, and said in a very soft voice: 'Marion! It's only me! You can come out now!' But there was no one there. I thought of myself helping her up the side of the quarry, telling the policeman to get an ambulance and tying my handkerchief round her head.

It was very quiet except for these shouts away in the distance. I could hear the people coming nearer as they beat their way through the ferns. I started to climb up the side of the quarry. I got to the top and through the trees and I could see the policeman and the others. I felt glad.

I walked round the quarry to the edge that went down like a cliff. The other quarry was only a few yards away and I went over and looked down into it. Then I went back to the far quarry, the one where me and Raymond Garnett had collected the stones that day. I looked down the sheer cliff. I had never been down that side before, only about two feet when Garno dared me that day.

Where I was standing, it sloped down for a few feet and then there was a tree growing out of the side of the quarry. I slithered down to the stump of the tree, getting hold of it with both hands. I looked down and it was a sheer drop to the bottom, but at the side of the tree you could just get your feet on a stone that jutted out and work your way down that way.

I tested the stone with my feet and got down on to it. There were bits of branch coming out of the side of the quarry, strong roots that you could get hold of. All the way down there were boulders and bits of stone jutting out where you could put your feet.

I worked my way slowly down. I didn't know why I was going down except that I had never been down this way before, and I couldn't do it when Garno dared me to. I clambered my way down to some bushes that grew near the bottom. There was a big clump of them, then a drop of about four feet, and then you reached another clump. I got to the first lot of bushes and started working my way further down, backwards. I kept slipping and I had to get hold of the branches. They were thorny and cut my hands so that I slipped still more with letting loose. I grabbed hold of the bush near the root to save myself, and sort of turned so that I could look down.

Marion was lying there, lying up against the side of the bushes. She lay with her head back over a stone. Her mouth and her eyes were open, and there was dried blood on her face. She wore the velvet dress that I liked so much, but it was all pulled up round her waist. I could imagine her saying: 'Oo, I'm showing all I've got!' and pulling it down again. But she didn't move.

I shouted: 'Mister! Mister! She's down here!' Some men ran to the top of the cliff and then the policeman came. I shouted again: 'She's down here!'

He started clambering down, quickly, using the branches of the trees the same as I had done. He got down to the bush where I was standing and slid down to where Marion was lying. He bent over her and listened to her chest. The other men were clambering down as well.

The policeman half stood up, holding himself by one of the branches. He took a whistle on a chain from out of his top pocket and started blowing it.

I felt proud and happy and sad and sick, all at the same time.

19

ALL that week-end we were all kept in, first in the house, then in the gardens, but never allowed out into the street.

All that Saturday morning we sat at the windows and watched people coming and going. Cars kept coming up to Longbottom's and detectives getting out. A policeman came down the street with Big Rayner and went into Longbottom's with him. After a bit they came out and went back up the street again. All the women in the street stood talking to each other at the garden gates.

We sat at the windows and started writing messages to each other. 'Got any American comics.' 'Don't stock them.' 'What time is it.' '5 and 20 past 11.' We put the messages in the windows for each to see. They were written on the backs of corn flakes boxes and on old bits of paper. Soon that game stopped and kids' mothers started letting them out of doors to swop comics with each other.

The sun was shining outside but it was like getting ready for a long, rainy day, taking comics out of the cupboard and sorting them into big piles and taking them from door to door, swopping—'Seen it'—'Seen it' —'Seen it'—but never going near Longbottom's.

When we were, after a long while, allowed out into Coronation Grove, nobody played games. We just went and stared at the police cars and the men coming out of Longbottom's until it was time to go in again.

At school on Monday it was just like a holiday. The bell didn't go for ages after nine o'clock, then we all trooped into the hall. After prayers, instead of going to the classrooms like we always did, we were just kept standing there. We stood and stood and then kids started talking and whispering. At first the teachers told them to shut up, but as the morning wore on they let us talk.

Nobody knew it was me who found Marion. The policeman had told me not to tell anyone at school, and my Auntie Betty said I would be sent away if I did. I knew nobody would believe me in any case.

'Bet they don't half get into cop it, whoever it was,' said Mono.

'They get hung,' another kid said.

'*They* don't. Not always,' Mono said.

The other kid said: 'They do, cos that feller that killed that woman, down where my grandma lives, well *he* got hung.' He was in 2C, this kid.

'Yer, well they don't hang everybody,' said Mono.

'How much do you bet?'

'I don't bet, but they don't.'

The kid out of 2C looked round and saw old Webby leaning against the parallel bars that we used for gym.

He whispered over in a hoarse shout: 'Sir! Sir!'

Old Webby looked towards him.

'Sir, don't they get hung for murder?'

'*They* don't, do they, sir?' said Mono. 'Not *every* time.'

'You boys shut up and look to the front!' snapped old Webby, suddenly straightening up.

'Told yer!' whispered Mono.

'Front!' shouted Webby. They shut up.

After a while old Croggy comes up and starts whispering to Webby. Old Webby walked up between the lines of boys and whispered something to Little Rayner. I heard him. He said: 'You'd better go off home, Rayner. Go straight home and don't talk to anybody on the way.'

Little Rayner had been standing there looking white and not talking to anybody. He walked out without saying anything.

'*He* didn't do it, did he, man?' whispered the kid from 2C.

'No, but their kid did!' whispered Mono.

At the front of the hall the teacher was marching the first class out. The second class marched out after them. What happened usually, Miss Priestly played the piano as we marched out, but she didn't today. We marched to our classroom in silence, except for the whisper that buzzed from line to line:

'Big Rayner's been taken away!'

In the playground that morning I found a quiet group of kids all standing round Raymond Garnett. He had fainted during assembly that morning—he was *al*ways blinking fainting—and on his way back from the cloakroom he had seen Big Rayner with a policeman and a man in a raincoat. He said Big Rayner was crying.

I didn't like the way Raymond Garnett was getting all the kids round him when it was *me* who found Marion Longbottom in the first place.

I said: 'Bet you don't know who found her.'

'Yar, well we do then,' said Raymond Garnett. 'It was that copper that lives down Parkside. See, swank pot!'

'Yar, well it wasn't then, cos it was me!' I said.

'Cur, listen to him!' shouted the kid out of 2C. 'Bet you knew just where to look, didn't you?'

Just then I saw one of the teachers standing on the edge of the group. He shouted: 'All right, you lads!' Then he went over to old Croggy's window that faced on to the playground. Old Croggy was leaning out of the window. He was always spying on us.

The teacher spoke to old Croggy and after a bit he came back a few steps and shouted of me and Raymond Garnett. We went over. Old Croggy shouted from his window: 'You boys go and help Mr Webb with the milk. And no chattering.'

We went and helped old Webby with the milk.

20

I ONLY went to look at Marion's grave once, just to see what it was like.

She was buried in the churchyard at Holy Hoss church. I went there one afternoon after Sunday-school. It was held in the cub hut in Wharfedale Avenue.

I had been planning to go all week. I looked sad all through Sunday-school and after a bit, just before the hymn, I asked the Sunday-school teacher if I could leave early. She asked me why.

'I've got to go to somebody's grave before I go home,' I said.

She gave me a funny look and said: 'Whose grave?'

'Just—somebody I used to know,' I said. I tried to put a catch in my voice, but I couldn't. I was nearly laughing, even though I didn't want to.

'Who?' said the Sunday-school teacher.

'Marion Longbottom,' I said.

The Sunday-school teacher gave me another funny look and said: 'Well, can't you go afterwards?' It was not the reply I was expecting and I felt mad at her.

I said: 'Ah, but I've got to go to my grandma's after.'

She said: 'Yes, well you'll be in plenty of time.' She was not sorry for me at all, and I had to wait till right after Sunday-school to go to the Holy Hoss churchyard.

I liked the graveyard, it was always so busy. I had

been looking forward to going all day and I was wearing my cub cap so that I could take it off when I got inside the churchyard gate.

I walked under the lych-gate and up the path towards the church door. There were a lot of people putting flowers on graves. I tried to look sad and I held my cap up in my hand so that everybody could see I had taken it off.

At the war memorial I stopped and looked for my father's name. The war memorial was a long pillar of white stone with all the names of the people who were killed in the war carved in gold. My father's name was not on it. He was not killed in the war. I was disappointed because his name was not there.

I was not sure which was Marion's grave so I walked round reading the tombstones. When anyone was watching I would stand by a tombstone and bite my lip and pucker my face, then I would heave a deep breath and walk away with my head held high, looking brave.

All the graves seemed to be big long ones, and two or three people seemed to be buried in each one. I saw Mono's father's grave. It was just like a little white plant pot with 'George Monoghan, April 8, 1898—October 17, 1937' on it painted in black. There were no flowers.

I walked round the side of the church and there was a new grave with some new planks over it, and a lot of old graves, all worn over with grass and weeds. I was frightened to walk on the grass in case I stood on somebody's grave.

Nearly at the back of the church I saw a newly-made grave that looked small enough for Marion. It was banked up like a coffin made out of dirt and it had a vase of white carnations on it. *Think* they were carnations.

I trod as carefully as I could along the grass verges and stood by the grave. It had a little wooden notice on it, like a label. All it said was: 'Gone to Little Jesus,' but there was no name or anything on it.

I thought to myself that this must be Marion's grave and if it wasn't it didn't really matter. There were some people looking after graves nearby. I put my cap down where they could see it and started arranging these flowers in the vase, even though they didn't need any arranging.

I was pleased because nobody told me to stop it. They must have thought it was my sister. I took out my handkerchief and tried to cry, but I couldn't. I knelt down at the side of the grave and started praying. 'Please God let Marion Longbottom be all right and if this is someone else, well *her* then, and let Marion Longbottom not be sorry she's dead and the same with everyone else in this graveyard and in all the other graveyards. And don't let me get nits in my hair, amen.' I always ended my prayers like that because my head was always tickling.

I prayed for Marion, but all the time I was wondering if the people in the churchyard were watching me. I looked at them through my eyes half-closed but they were too busy looking after their own graves. I was pleased because they thought it was all right that I should be kneeling here and praying.

I got up and wandered as sadly as I could to the door of the church. I went inside. There were one or two people kneeling in some of the pews. I tiptoed down the aisle to nearly the front row and sat in one of the pews myself. I didn't kneel but sat with my head bowed. I closed my eyes and thought of the vicar coming up and putting his hand on my shoulder and asking me if he could do anything.

I stood up and walked out of the church, hoping I looked white. As I went out I opened my hand over the offertory box, trying to look as though I had put something in. I went back to Marion's grave—I *think* it was Marion's grave—and this time I did not kneel down but just stood there and gave it a long and sorry look. Then I turned and walked away down the path. I dabbed at my eyes with my handkerchief again, and tried to cry.

At the lych-gate I sat down on the stone seat and pretended to be sobbing. I was thinking to myself of women tiptoeing past and saying: 'No, leave him alone, he's all right,' but no women came past.

I tried to cry and I couldn't. I started thinking of sad things to *make* me cry. I thought of all the stray cats who were out at night, birds that had their beaks squashed in and couldn't peck, a lady tramp we used to see called Woodbine Lizzie who never had anything to eat. I thought about myself being dead and everybody being sorry. And then I started thinking of the saying that Marion had once told me: One for sorrow, two for joy, three for a letter, four for a boy, five for silver, six for gold, seven for a secret never to be told.

After a bit the slow tears came, but they were not for Marion or for anyone else so far as I knew.

21

As for Uncle Mad, I only ever once saw him again. It was getting dark nights now. The August Bank Holiday was over and out in the street it was getting crisp and exciting, like a parcel. The lamps were already lit at bedtime and it was nice to get in and sit round the fire with the *Dandy*, saved up all day specially.

The leaves were coming off the trees and down in the park the kids were beginning to fly kites up and down. A lot of them had box kites.

One night I was going to the park to look at them when I saw Mono at the top of our street. He was sitting on the railings watching the trams go past. I was eating toffee and I knew he would want some.

He saw me chewing and shouted after me: 'What have you got, man?'

I said: 'Everlasting. Do you want some?'

Mono jumped down off the railings and I pulled him off a piece of everlasting. He started walking beside me.

'Where are you going—the park?' he said.

'Yer.'

'So am I.'

He wasn't really, he was just sitting there on the railings but he thought he could get some more everlasting if he came with me. Just like Mono.

We walked on down Parkside.

'Big Rayner's been taken to that reform school,' said Mono after a bit.

'Poor old him,' I said. 'How long do they keep them there?'

'Till they're grown up,' said Mono. We were passing our school. 'They get the cane every day,' he said.

'Wouldn't like to be in *his* shoes,' I said.

'Neither would I,' said Mono. 'I think they wear grey uniforms.'

We turned into the park gates. The road that led down through the park was scattered with brown leaves. We started shuffling through them. The air was keen and fresh. Faintly we could hear the shouts from the swings and the slide and the cup and saucer, far down below us at the bottom of the park.

'Bet Big Rayner wishes he was here,' said Mono.

'Bet Marion Longbottom does as well,' I said.

'Yer. Poor old her,' said Mono.

He picked up a dock-leaf and started pulling it apart to make a harp out of the veins of the leaf. I took a rhododendron leaf. It was shiny and brittle and going brown at the edges. I could break bits off it.

'Have we to go through that pipe?' said Mono.

He wanted to go through this drainpipe at the other side of the park, where it leads through to the slag-heaps and all these sooty houses. *I* didn't want to blinking go. I thought he would try blocking it up when I got half-way through it.

I said: 'Yer.' I couldn't say anything else. There must have been another way through to the slag-heaps besides the pipe, but we never knew where it was. We walked on until we came to the pipe. It was like brown pot. You couldn't see to the other end because it curved in the middle.

'You first,' said Mono.

I got on my hands and knees and went into the pipe. You had to crawl along with your head down. At the bottom of the pipe there was a thin layer of dried mud, grey and cracked. I heard Mono coming behind me, going: 'Cur, isn't it narrow?' I was glad to hear his voice, but I was gladder still when I turned round the curve and I could see the light at the other end. I thought to myself, only a bit more, don't let them brick it up, we'll be out in a minute, they won't have time to brick it up now.

We got out at the other side and there were the slag-heaps and the pit nearby with a big wheel like at the Feast. Sometimes you saw men coming home with helmets on and their faces all black. The houses were in little streets with washing lines reaching from one house to another across the street. At the end of every street there were big posters for Oxydol, and little picture houses we had never been to. We could only tell we were in the same town by the buses, all of them the same colour as our own.

'Have we to go up to them new buildings?' said Mono. Far up at the top of the road where we came out they were putting up some new houses. They looked all new and clean and my heart sank whenever I saw them because they were like the houses in our own street, corporation houses with front doors that seemed to be grinning through their letter boxes. It seemed that houses like ours were springing up all over the world.

We walked up the steep road to the top where they were building. Some of the houses were finished. They had white stuff all over the windows and piles of sand in the gardens.

The road was all dug up here, and the causeway edge was about a foot deep. Next to the first new house we saw they had put up a notice, a street-sign that said: 'Parkside.' I suddenly realized that this must be the same Parkside that we knew, leading past our school and all the way round the park, and that you could get here that way instead of through the drainpipe. I was sorry because I wanted this place where the slag-heaps were to be somewhere you could only reach by crawling through this drainpipe in the park.

Further down the road some men were working on a patch of ground. They were digging a sort of trench and all round them there were sinks and baths covered in dirt and straw, and doors for the new houses, painted pale pink. We went to watch them. Suddenly Mono shouted out: 'Hey, look, man! There's that feller!'

I looked at each man, and I saw that one of them was Uncle Mad. He was wearing old blue trousers and a vest and he was swinging this big pick. He had like a snake tattoed down his arm. I had never seen his bare arms before. I had never thought of him working for a living.

He seemed altogether different. I had the same feeling as I had when I saw the street-sign saying: 'Parkside' and finding out that there was another way here besides through the pipe.

Mono shouted: 'Hiya, Uncle Mad!'

Uncle Mad made no sign. He did not even seem to hear. He was not smiling. His face was creased with watching what he was doing, swinging his pick into this big trench. He went on digging, along with the other men.

'Make that noise, Uncle Mad!' shouted Mono. But Uncle Mad would not look up. Mono picked up a small stone and threw it, lightly so as not to hurt. It caught Uncle Mad on the leg. One of the other workmen looked up and saw us.

'Gerraway, cheeky young devils!' he shouted.

We were standing near one of the sinks that were covered in earth and straw.

'Can we have that sink, Uncle Mad?' shouted Mono.

Uncle Mad still took no notice. The man who had shouted called out: 'I'll sink *you* if I've to come over there!'

Mono shouted: '*Give* us it! *Will* yer?'

Uncle Mad went on swinging his pick, looking neither to right nor left.

'We're taking it, Uncle Mad!' shouted Mono, making as if to get hold of the sink.

The man who had shouted dropped his pick and started chasing us. We ran down the road and ducked through the pipes, crawling quickly, thinking he was still after us. We piled out at the park end, but he had gone.

'He's daft, that feller!' said Mono as we stood, sniffling and giggling at the other end of the pipe.

'Who, Uncle Mad?' I said.

'Yer.'

That was the last time Uncle Mad was mentioned. We never saw him again.

We walked up the park road, between the rhododendrons. Again we could hear the shouts of all the kids playing. We walked down the path worn in the grass towards the swings and the slide and the cup and saucer. Mono jumped on the cup and saucer and started slurring his feet on the ground to stop it. All the kids on it shouted: 'La-ay off, man!' He got off and jumped on the foot swings and started making them go so high that the girls screamed.

I stood and watched. Nearby was the lake. It was busy with fishing nets and little boats called Ned, Tom and Dick. The three kids from the Catholic school, Spenco, Peggo and young Gin'er were just coming up from the lake towards the wooden shelter by the swings. Young Gin'er saw me as they went past. 'Hiya, thingy,' he said. They could not remember my name. They went in the shelter and started putting their fingers through the spyholes in the wood.

Across the lake I could see Ted, Little Rayner, Raymond Garnett and them in a little cluster. They were walking slowly along the path that led down towards the golf links. Up on the foot swings, Mono saw them too.

He shouted: 'Hey, look, man, there's the others! Bet they're off finding golf balls!'

With a wild jump he landed on the ground, leaving the foot swing creaking and the girls all screaming. Scrambling up Mono put his hand to his mouth and made an Indian yodel. He shouted: 'Ray-no! Gar-no! Wait on!'

Little Rayner and Ted looked round. 'Come on, man!' shouted Ted. '*Ru-un!*'

Mono started to run towards them. They all turned to wait for him. Little Rayner started taking off a runner puffing for breath.

188

I watched the crowd of them turn and walk towards the golf links. Little Rayner was singing: 'There was an old farmer had an old sow, how, sow, aye-diddle-ow' at the top of his voice. His voice carried through the park long after they had gone. I walked slowly up the hill towards the park gates. It was still crisp and chilly. Looking down into the park it seemed unreal because the air was so steady. The voices of the last lot of kids on the slide and on the lake carried up the hill towards me. In Parkside, a lamp flickered and went on by itself.

I sat on the low wall by the gates for a long time, listening to the shouts that kept coming up from the park. It began to get cold, and I started thinking of a fire at home and the comics and new cake and that. I got up and started to walk up Parkside.

Passing our school I saw that the lights were on in the classrooms. I looked in our classroom and there were a lot of big lads sitting on the desks and standing round talking. It was enrolment night for night school. They all looked happy and important, knowing that they didn't have to *sit* at the desks like we did.

There was a lump in my throat, suddenly. It was not the kind of lump I forced on myself by thinking sad thoughts on purpose. It just happened on its own, and I did not want it.

I turned down our street. The sky had suddenly gone dark and there was the first pit-pat of rain. The sharpness went out of the air and the rain began to fall. I looked up and shouted, even though there was nobody with me: 'Rain, rain, go away, come again another day!' I was glad of the rain because it hid the tears on my face.

I reached our house and the lights were on. Through the window I could see my Auntie Betty peering out at the rain. She saw me and beckoned for me to come in. She was smiling, in a way. It began to rain faster. I rubbed a hand over my eyes and ran indoors.

KEITH WATERHOUSE

BIMBO

Grossly misrepresented in her ghosted memoirs, Page Three glamour girl Debra Chase determines to set the record straight. Here then is the truth about her dizzy rise to fame via Tulse Hill's most revered fashion school, her liaisons with the entire Seathorpe soccer team and the lecherous Sir Monty Pratt MP, and her ensuing downfall. With sardonic wit and compassionate insight, Keith Waterhouse has composed a masterpiece of characterisation and a wickedly entertaining satire on contemporary British society.

'A great tragi-comedy . . . this book is up there in lights with the funniest, the saddest and the best novels in English. It is wrought by a massive intelligence operating an exquisite and lacerating sense of irony'
Peter Mullen in the Daily Mail

'A treat for sore brains'
Patrick Skene Catling in The Spectator

'Hilarious . . . with a ring of authenticity in every gleeful and sleazy line'
Celia Brayfield in She

'It takes a hugely skilled wordsmith to make a banal world like Debra Chase's such compulsive reading . . . Read. Enjoy'
Miles Kington in The Literary Review

sceptre